THE MERMAID CALL

ALEX COTTER

nosy
crow

For Laurie

First published in the UK in 2022 by Nosy Crow Ltd
The Crow's Nest, 14 Baden Place
Crosby Row, London, SE1 1YW, UK

Nosy Crow Eireann Ltd
44 Orchard Grove, Kenmare
Co Kerry, V93 FY22, Ireland

ISBN: 978 1 83994 190 0

A CIP catalogue record for this book is available from the
British Library.

Printed and bound in the UK by Clays Ltd, Elcograf S.p.A.
Typeset by Tiger Media

Papers used by Nosy Crow are made from wood grown in
sustainable forests

MIX
Paper from
responsible sources
FSC® C018072
www.fsc.org

1 3 5 7 9 10 8 6 4 2

www.nosycrow.com

Prologue

Whose mirror have you been looking in?

Mimi's question was swimming through my head as I stared at my reflection in the oily surface of the pond; shiny greens, blues and pinks from the minerals feeding the cave.

Whose mirror have you been looking in, Vivien?

It was the question Mimi – my gran – asked whenever I turned on myself ("too ugly", "too curly", "*two* big feet").

As if the answer could be my way out.

The darkly coloured water seemed to shiver. I glanced sharply back around our new prison, from its star-studded black ceiling to the shadowy rock ledge behind me. Lit only by the glow from my head-torch, my new friend was lying as still as Sleeping Beauty. Waiting for her wish to come true. It sent a fiercer surge of panic hurtling through me, a greyhound after a rabbit: *she needs help!* I began lowering myself into the pond, legs immediately starting a frenzied doggy-paddle – it was deep and cold; lake-cold. Fixing my eyes on a shaft of grey liquid light beneath the water, I prepared to dive: torso stretching; arms pointing; fingers together in an arrow. A tankful of air into my lungs, and … I sliced through the water; deep, deep down.

Water's my ally. In water I can be dainty and delicate; fast and fierce. I can be anything I want to be. Water turns me as regal as a swan. In water I can be a shark, a dolphin … a mermaid. Except – my hands immediately met an ice-cold wall of resistance. Now water was the enemy. Like an army of serpentine soldiers I had to fight; a witch I had to foil, or she'd cook us in a cauldron of frog legs and fish eyes. My heart sped up. The lake wanted to keep us here, trapped for eternity.

I could already sense my lungful of oxygen leaking, straining for air from the pit of my stomach. A faster kick of legs, a stronger sweep of my arms; deeper still into the cold, wet darkness. The water kept pushing and slapping as, eyes stinging, I swam on, to fight those serpentine soldiers, escape the cauldron-witch.

To reach another world.

Whose mirror have you been looking in?

I knew the answer. I knew now whose story I had been trapped inside.

Welcome to Lake Splendour

There has long been a tale of a freshwater mermaid at Lake Splendour. Invading Romans thought she was the goddess Amphitrite. From the twelfth century, there was talk of a vengeful Lake Mermaid, called Melusine, haunting their waters. When village fisherfolk discovered a queen conch shell at the bottom of the lake, they took it as proof she existed. They used the shell to beg the Lake Mermaid for miracles and mercy; for fish, not the floods and fog that plagued their livelihoods.

Then, in 1914, two 15-year-old village girls, Lydia and Violet, declared the Lake Mermaid spoke to them through the ancient queen conch shell. Soon after, they completely vanished. On their return, months later, the girls claimed they had been summoned by the powerful Lake Mermaid, who was fighting for a better world where mermaids ruled beyond the water. They said the Lake Mermaid had sent them back to help with the Great War on land, and they would rejoin her once the battles of men were done.

Alas, they would never return to her. When the trenches took the lives and limbs of so many of Lake

Splendour's workers, it was Lydia and Violet who stepped in, using their tale of meeting the great and powerful Lake Mermaid to single-handedly save the village by encouraging visitors to come and spot the legendary mermaid for themselves.

Known as the Mermaid Girls ever since, they led a movement of tradeswomen to build the tourist trade you see today: from hotels and tearooms to boat trips and mermaid arts and crafts (we even have mermaid fruit and veg!). People from far and wide continue to visit to seek their own Lake Mermaid adventure! What will yours look like?

We wish you a very warm and watery welcome to Lake Splendour!

©Lake Splendour Tourist Office

Mum's Homecoming
Two Weeks Earlier

Hair. I suppose you could say it all started with hair: short, long, glossy, greasy, straight, wavy, curly – *very curly.*

Hair. It's what I think of first when I picture Mum. And right then Mum was all I was thinking about. She was arriving that very evening! My stomach could not stop *whizz-pop-banging.* After three years of *might be, would she, why hasn't she?* Mum was coming home to

Lake Splendour – her and her fairytale silk.

Hair. It's what greets me first when I reflection. Mum's crowning glory bypassed m   have thick and wild, sort-of-toffee-coloured, tight coils of curls that never – *ever!* – grow past my shoulders (I have tried; I have tried very hard). My hair is the first thing people notice about me (I wish it wasn't), and *not* in the way people notice Mum's. I get whispers, a lot, behind my back; sometimes fingers reach out to touch. I have to act like I don't notice, or that I don't mind, or *ha-ha, that's so funny*, when they snigger, "She's been electrified!" or "Check out the bird's nest!" *again.*

I'd asked Mimi, my gran, that morning if I could buy some hair straighteners for Mum's homecoming ("No way, no chance!" she'd said), and I was trying to think of other ways to tame my frizz, when Eleni clicked her fingers.

"Are you listening, Vivien?"

Hair. It's what Eleni had done to hers that was still bothering me. She'd chopped her black mane off to her chin last Saturday and I'd been sitting opposite Imposter Eleni all week. The worst part was she'd not told me she was going to do it, when we share if we're planning to trim our toenails! Well, we used to. Eleni was changing.

"I said Hero invited us to sit with them – the MPs."
Eleni was pointing tentatively across the school canteen
to the table where the Mighty Protestors were sat: badge-
wearing Hero; Jadon and his nose stud; Emma with the
diamanté eye patch; Khalil, who wore mascara; and
Skye with the blue-tipped braids. Older, cooler students
with rebellious twists to their uniforms and confident,
podium-loud opinions. Frankly, they were scary.

"Nope, I prefer it here," I said, and stabbed a soggy,
fat chip with my fork.

"But it's the last day of term. Wouldn't it be fun to join
them?"

Fun? I nearly choked on my chip. As fun as being
forced to take maths GCSE four years early. No
way could I sit with the MPs and pretend to be cool,
rebellious, confident. I was useless at pretending.

"Hero is amazing." Eleni was still gazing misty-eyed
in her direction.

My stomach shrank a little. It had not escaped my
notice that Eleni's new hair was a mirror-copy of Hero's.
(And yes, that *is* her real name.) She had been kissing the
ground *All-hail-Hero* walked on ever since she led our
climate change march a few months ago. Eleni no longer
seemed to care about our own campaigns – *Improve
School Dinners!* and *Oi, Stop Your Littering!* "Childish",

she'd called them yesterday.

"We talked for ages when Hero came in for her battered haddock last night." Eleni pushed her glasses up her nose. "She wants me to get more active with the MPs."

I sat back so hard my canteen chair bounced. *That's it!* I had an urge to grab a fistful of Hero's badge-filled jacket and remind her: *Eleni Christofi is* my *best friend, not yours.* Huh, like I'd dare. I had a doctor's note the day they gave out backbones. I shifted lower in my seat; I'm your keep-the-peace-and-everyone-happy type of person. *Nice, polite,* teachers report (plus "should speak up more"). I never argue with anyone, never fall out with Mimi, not one row with Eleni in all the years we've been best friends; I'm even pleasant to cold-callers. There should be a bone for that.

Eleni was making that chewing face, when she's not sure how to say something, until: "The MPs are anti-mermaid." She said it really quickly, like pulling off a plaster with words.

"What? How can anyone live here and not love mermaids!" I was aware I was spluttering, but *blimey* – Lake Splendour *exists* because of our annual Mermaid Festival. It's bigger than Christmas round these parts. There's a costume parade with fancy floats and a park funfair and the Lake Race. And it was all happening in just two weeks' time.

"The MPs want the Mermaid Crown to be stopped," Eleni replied hesitantly.

"Never!" I drew a breath like she'd just uttered the worst swear word ever. "The Crown is the heart of the whole festival!"

You get to enter if you're a girl between nine and sixteen, and you win this amazing crown. (That's *you* as in *everyone-you* … not *me*.) But the *biggest* thing is the crowned mermaid gets her picture in the national newspapers. It's how we keep tourists coming.

Eleni was screwing up her nose like there was a bad smell. "Don't you think the Mermaid Crown is really, really sexist?"

I shook my head quickly. "Boys can enter to win King Neptune's trident."

"It's not the same, Vivien." Eleni took off her glasses as if she wanted me to go blurry. "Hero says the Mermaid Crown is just a beauty pageant for girls."

"Err, not true. It's judged on a *really* good costume." Wig. Tail. Shell accessories. The usual.

"Then why is it always the popular, pretty girls who win?" Eleni retorted. She flicked her head back at our year's Princess Table behind us: a poster for the Mermaid

Crown if ever there was one. Not one of them was a Curly. Not one had my broad swimmer's shoulders. They all had small feet ("Where *did* you get your size sevens from, Vivien?" *Thanks, Mimi*). The Princess Table all had long hair (*they* were allowed straighteners!) and no spots (witchcraft; must be), and our blue tartan school skirt looked sleek on them, not potato-sack. I picked at mine and added weakly, "But the Mermaid Crown is a festival tradition."

"Hero says traditions are just an excuse not to change. She says mermaids were invented by the pat-ri-archy." Eleni stumbled over that last word. Then she closed her eyes, like I wouldn't understand.

My shrunken stomach shrivelled. *All-hail-Hero.* I stared down at my plate of soggy, fat chips and greasy, thin gravy that – *actually* – really did need *Improve School Dinners!*, before I said quietly, "Yeah, but we *sell* mermaids. We *need* the Mermaid Crown." That's *we* as in my family's shop, Enchanted Tails. "If we don't make enough from the tourists this summer, we might go bust."

Mimi said we'd had the worst year ever for takings; we were already more hard up than usual. I was having to wear last year's blue anorak (already second-hand) because Mimi couldn't afford to buy me one of those trendy puffer jackets everyone else has. Museums would soon be queuing up to put my phone on display. My stomach grew some lumpy potatoes to fill my potato-sack skirt.

"Sorry, I know mermaids matter more to you," I heard Eleni sigh. This time we both went eyes-to-our-plate quiet. The high-pitched shrieks from Princess Table seemed to get louder. "So what time's your mum getting here?"

I looked up again, relieved. Eleni's eyes were doing an olive branch. "After seven-ish tonight!" (Everything was an *ish* with Mum.) "We can pause *Improve School Dinners!* if you want, prioritise *Oi, Stop Your Littering!*" I could compromise. Mum was all that mattered right now.

Mum was finally coming home.

So, I'd not seen Mum in three years. Which, *yup*, is a massively long time not to see your nearest and dearest, I know, but you have to understand: Mum's a free spirit. Mimi says she was born flying. ("Whoosh, out of the womb!"). She flew away from Lake Splendour well before I was born and again after she'd had me. "Like a stork: delivered you, then took off." Mimi would flap her arms like it was no big deal.

Mimi says she's afraid Mum will never be able to settle in one place, which is why she's had to raise me. Mimi might be my gran ("Don't you ever call me Gran!") but I suppose she's more like another mum; she's even the same age as some of my friends' parents. She's beautiful like Mum is, just a little more lined and saggy … and strict.

Mum, the stork, works on cruise ships. She's forever travelling to exotic locations, so it's not her fault she can't see me all that much. She always writes *Wish you were here* on the postcards stuck to our fridge. And every birthday I get a mermaid doll from all over the world. We're talking:

Hawaiian mo'o

Estonian näkk

South American oriyu

Sirena of the Philippines

Japanese ningyo

West Africa's Igbagbo and Yemoja

South Africa's Kaaiman

I keep them lined up on the shelf above my bed even though Eleni says they creep her out ("They're plotting something"). So what if they are: they're beautiful and Mum chose each one, parcelled it up, stuck on a postage stamp. So every one, I treasure.

I'd already made my usual peel-off from Eleni at the shopping precinct. We'd not mentioned *All-hail-Hero* and her anti-mermaid views again. It wasn't worth losing my best friend over. Plus, it's not like I don't have a number-two friend as well. That's Erik. He's in my swim club and he's the best at somersault dives.

I continued down Lake Mermaid Road alone. It's only me who lives right at the lakefront, above our shop. Eleni lives above her family chippy, Poseidon. It started as a Greek Cypriot restaurant, then Eleni's mum and dad realised tourists form bigger queues for fish and chips than for their famed chicken souvlaki (even though their souvlaki is *DE-licious*). Most kids from my school live on the modern estates higher up the hill, in those look-a-like houses I've always envied because they have gardens big enough for trampolines and parents who mostly come in twos and cars fit for families.

I passed by Fin's Waves, where the old ladies envy my natural curls (yes, you heard right; old ladies fashion their perms on me. Now do you feel my pain?). I was busy comforting myself with a mental list of all the things Mum and I could do together, what with summer holidays starting tomorrow. Headed *Keep it fun for Mum* because I think she gets bored easily. She's used to excitement, thrills, see? I reckoned if I could make it really exciting, she might not fly away too soon.

Maybe not ever again? (*Double whizz-pop-bang.*)

On past Nature's Bounty, our fruit and veg shop. In tourist season they showcase their daily produce that "most resembles a mermaid". Today's: knobbly turnip with a flick of a hairy tail. Past Neptune's Inn (Mum often stays there. She needs her "own space") and Splash Tearooms (serving the best conch cream horns). Even our bank has a shell-framed cash machine, and don't get me started on our fishmonger's or we'd be here all day (mermaid-scale mussels, anyone?).

It started drizzling as I passed the shell shop (Conch Curios) and the sky had turned the same mournful ash-grey as our village slate and stone. I pulled up my anorak hood to protect my hair from the frizzies. Lake Splendour is as north as you can go in England before you become Scottish. It rains *a lot* (hence trusty anorak) and even on summer days the sun hardly ever wants to get its hat on. But today – I hugged Mum's visit tightly to my chest like it was Christmas Eve – the sun (wherever it had gone) might as well be dressed in rainbow brightness.

I paused to happily pick up a crisp wrapper and put it in the bin. Fact: we lose countless lake birds to the perils of littering. Our village council spends more on litter-picking than libraries! Chew on that, *All-hail-Hero*.

At the bottom of the road and there it is: the postcard shot of our lake. Silvery water topped by majestic green and grey craggy mountains and flanked by sloping hills of fir trees on either side. Follow the path round to the right of the water and you soon reach our Shell Grotto and the Illuminated Cave where the village's famous Mermaid Girls, Lydia and Violet, said they met the Lake Mermaid in 1914. Ever since, people have been visiting the cave to try their luck at capturing that million-dollar mermaid photo, you know, like they do with the Loch Ness Monster or Bigfoot or the Abominable Snowman.

Along the lakefront, mermaid bunting had been strung up between the cast-iron lampposts in readiness for our week-long Mermaid Festival. In a fortnight there'd be wooden huts lining our wide promenade, selling chocolate mermaid tails and edible shell necklaces; plastic crowns and tridents; long nylon wigs galore. The first Saturday of the festival launches the Mermaid Crown: colourful floats leading a parade of girls dressed as mermaids to snag the sparkly tiara, and (not so many) boys kitted out to win Neptune's trident. The crowning and trident-ing takes place on the Sunday in the Shell Grotto. A week of funfair and fireworks, and the festival closes the following Saturday with the Lake Race. I was finally old enough to swim in it this year. And Mum just *had* to stay for it! You see, if my mum had been given wings, I'd got fins. My insides tickled – maybe Mum would even watch me win the race! *Triple whizz-pop-bang.* OK, so it was the Mermaid Crown that Mum won when she was my age, not a swimming race, but maybe I could prove to her I was good at something, that I was worth visiting. I pictured myself stepping up to the podium to receive the trophy, Mum bouncing up and down and clapping the hardest of anyone. "My brilliant daughter!" she'd squeal.

The image sent me flying past the row of lace-curtained bed and breakfasts (Mermaid's Rest; Siren Slumbers), all of them displaying mermaid-shaped *Vacancies* signs (one or two with accompanying dead flies). I whizzed by Atlantis Arcades with its flashing mermaid lights and piped music, until, *there*, just before the lake curves back up towards the mountains – Enchanted Tails. I had to hurry and change in case Mum was (miraculously) early. I planned on wearing the dungaree dress and stripy top Mimi got me last Christmas. My stomach twisted: was it grown up enough for Mum? I'd already decided to put my hair up (last time Mum made a comment about it being too bushy and bothersome). Maybe I could sneak

17

a spray of Mimi's knock-off Chanel (Mum also said I always stink of chlorine).

It's fair to say my stomach was now *whizz-pop-banging* like the festival fireworks. I didn't know how I was going to keep calm till she arrived! Mimi was in the shop window arranging a new display of children's mermaid costumes on cut-out card mannequins. I drew up to the glass, squashing my nose against it and raising monster claws to make Mimi laugh. Mimi has the same conker-brown hair as Mum, though she never bothers with make-up or fancy clothes; just her usual rope plait and tattered, green lace-up boots.

She spotted me.

She didn't laugh.

Her mouth was drawn into a thin line like she was gripping a row of sewing pins between her lips.

Straightaway, my stomach dropped like an anchor. I knew that look well, the same look when Belle our ancient gerbil died a year ago; the same look she had the last time Mum was supposed to be coming.

Which meant I already knew what she was going to shout through the glass even before she opened her mouth. I looked away, back at the lake, a sudden urge to plunge into the cold water, anything to get away from—

"Your mum called. I'm sorry, Vivien. She's cancelled again."

My dreams of summer fizzed and dissolved like some cheap chemistry experiment.

I refocused my eyes on the window. From Mimi and her shiny plait to my own reflection: frizzy hair and broad shoulders.

Mum wasn't coming – because I just wasn't good enough.

Alice DeLacey

"What are you all looking at?"

I cast evils round the shop the next day, at every single one of them. And there are many, believe me, lined up on every shelf, assembled *oh-so prettily* across every table: mermaids, merrows, selkies, sirens, river nymphs, water sprites, kelpies, nixies and naiads. Hundreds of magical, mystical figures in plastic, fabric, clay, china, wool – all of them staring back at me with unfazed, unblinking eyes, and all of them *smug*.

I rubbed at my own eyes. They were still stinging, like there was crushed glass beneath my lids. Hot and swollen and red-sore from all the crying.

"Oh, lovey, sobbing yourself to sleep won't make her magically appear," Mimi had cooed as she passed my door on a late-night loo trip.

"She'll never change, your mum," she'd said gently over breakfast, sitting at the small table in our tiny kitchen with its view across the lake. Saturday doorstop toast, which usually I wolf down, but nothing could get past the humongous lump of disappointment in my throat.

"You have to accept the way she is or else she'll be forever letting you down," Mimi said, wearing that pained look of hers: mouth folded, forehead criss-crossed with worry lines.

It made me do my best to smooth out my own frowns, to wear the please-Mimi smile I employ on school photos. Because even framed in a strip of morning sunshine, Mimi was looking weary and troubled. I bet she'd been hoping to see Mum too.

"Err, did you not hear me?' I said, sweeping my gaze back round scores of unblinking, mocking eyes in our small shop. "It's rude to stare!" Hanging from the ceiling, spilling from trunks on the floor, shelves upon

21

shelves upon shelves of beautiful creatures.

I was keeping shop while Mimi was at a festival committee meeting, then the bank. The last Saturday of every month she deposits money in a savings account for my future. Mimi has high hopes for me. "You'll be the first in our family to go to university!" She wants me to come back with a certificate to prove I've got a brain, like Dorothy's scarecrow in *The Wizard of Oz*. She wants me to grow Enchanted Tails into an Elon Musk empire. I want that too, but with Mum by my side, like you see businesses with *Someone & Son*.

I prodded one of the soft fabric mermaid dolls sitting beside our ancient brass till. "You think you're sooooo special." Blue and green and pink shimmery tails, *long* hair in different shades: black, brown, blonde. Nothing vaguely toffee-coloured, shoulders-short or frizzy. I made a fist and punched them each on their perfect button noses so they toppled drunkenly across the counter, right as the bell above the door went. It makes a sound like Tinkerbell – a bit silly, but Mimi always defends it with "The tourists want magic!" I straightened up professionally and tidied the mermaid dolls, stretching my mouth into my practised welcome-smile (a close relation to my school-photo-smile). Mimi's trusted me to manage the shop on my own for nearly a year now.

She says it's good for my confidence.

A woman with two small girls in identical purple coats began wandering round. They examined our rail of mermaid costumes before making oohs and aahs over the dolls. I held my welcome-smile, even though it was starting to ache.

"That's the one I want. She's really beautiful, Mummy." The smaller girl started stroking the shiny hair of our largest mermaid.

"Just like you, Rosie," the mum said, stroking her daughter's hair like she was a doll too. Then: "Polly, how many times? Stand up straighter," she snapped at the older girl (straggly bunches and a scab on her chin) and within a flash of a mermaid's tail the mum was ushering them out again, a hushed mumble about checking out the doll on Amazon. We get a lot of those browse-and-buy-onliners.

My shoulders had already sloped in solidarity with straggly Polly; my professional welcome-smile was for nothing. They'd not even noticed me. I sneaked a glance at the wall behind, at the framed picture there of my mum getting crowned Festival Mermaid 2001 – when she was nearly thirteen, like me – a sudden clawing erupting in my chest with a memory of her voice: "*I always thought my daughter would look more like me.*" It was something I overheard Mum saying to Mimi on her last visit, three years ago. I'd stored it in the murky depths of my mind like tinned vegetables at the back of the cupboard. Occasionally I tried to reshape it like putty so it wouldn't hurt so much. But now it was growing monstrously – past the (still humongous) lump of disappointment in my throat – as swollen and sticky as candyfloss on a stick. *Would Mum want to visit me if I did look more like her?*

"*Yes!*" the mermaids, merrows, selkies, sirens, river nymphs, water sprites, kelpies, nixies and naiads seemed to nod in unison. "*Yes, of course she would, stupid!*"

I scowled at them, squeezing my sore eyes shut against new tears, just as Tinkerbell announced another customer. I didn't even bother to look up this time, never mind plaster on my welcome-smile. I punched the soft mermaids again (far too pleased with themselves) and collapsed my head like a block of concrete on to the counter. I was even starting to think maybe Eleni's precious Hero had cause to be anti-Mermaid (*Wash your mouth out, Vivien!*), when I heard the soft sound of snivelling – followed by those donkey-braying noises when you're trying really hard not to cry. I'd made enough of those last night.

I drew myself up and crept quietly along the counter.

Peering round the middle shelves I saw a sunshine-coloured head crouching by our ceramic naiad wishing dolls – a head that was crying, *a lot*.

I cleared my throat loudly. Two eyes glanced up. Hers looked even redder than mine felt. She began blinking quickly – crushed glass too then.

"Are you OK?" I said cautiously. She was about my age; I recognised her as the posh granddaughter of the old DeLacey couple who live in the la-di-da house high above the lake.

The girl sniffed loudly and made a sound like "eurgh". One hand casually caressed a naiad wishing doll before she rose towards the counter, arms loose at her side, feet in front of one another, like she was on a catwalk.

Wow. Up close she was even lovelier; not Princess Table, but pretty in a different way. Deep-sea-blue eyes set wide apart, a curiously shaped parcel-bow mouth, and this aloof expression like she was staring out of a fancy painting at the world. I flicked another look at the picture of Mum getting crowned Mermaid, while a second candyfloss-sticky thought went charging through my mind, like a bull in a china (mermaid) shop: *If I looked like this girl I bet Mum wouldn't cancel.*

"No, I'm not OK, not really." The vision of beauty was shaking her head. Her silky hair swished with the gesture, not rigid like mine. Then she burst into a torrent of tears, as loud and fast as a waterfall.

I stretched out an arm, retrieved it and rubbed my neck awkwardly. "Um, why, what's the matter?"

A deep jagged breath. The girl made a little motion with her neck to stem her crying, gulped and said, "It's complicated," in a voice as la-di-da as her grandparents' house.

"Err, well, do you want to sit down?" I indicated the purple scallop-shell beanbag beneath the window, which is my go-to place to read when the shop is closed and Mimi's hogging the TV in our small lounge. The out-of-a-painting DeLacey girl bobbed her wet, pink face. I made a grab for the box of tissues beneath the counter.

"Things will seem better by tomorrow," I said, copying what Mimi told me last night, as the girl settled herself down. I offered her the tissues and sat cross-legged at her feet.

"I don't think they will," she sniffed, then: *hic*. A trail of glistening snot was streaming out of her nose – and she STILL LOOKED PRETTY!

I fidgeted. "D'you want to talk about it?" I felt bad for her, but all right, I'll admit I was curious too.

Out-of-a-painting clenched and unclenched her hands – her fingers were the only imperfect part of her: scraped and cut, like she'd fallen over. "The Dragon – that's my grandma – just got really mad at me." *Hic.* The deep-sea eyes squeezed out more tears. "It wasn't my choice to stay with them, but after I got—" She paused abruptly, like she was going to say something she shouldn't. She wiped a tissue under her nose and blinked her eyes several times. "Never mind."

I shifted closer. "Why did your grandma get mad?" Mimi can be strict about doing homework and chores and not moaning ("Think of the starving children, Vivien!"), but she never gets really cross. Like I said, never a bad word between us.

Another wet hiccup. "She found me in my dead aunt's room."

Err – "Your dead aunt's room?" That wasn't what I was expecting.

Sniff. "The Dragon – she keeps it like a museum."

"Oh." I didn't really know what else to say. Everyone knew the old DeLacey couple had two daughters. One was this girl's mum. The other one had drowned in the lake when she was about my age, during a Mermaid Festival. But no one really talked about it. Because it happened twenty years ago and involved mermaid-searching, and the village wouldn't want tourists getting a whiff of tragedy that might spoil the magic.

Hic. "She caught me with my Aunt Stella's diary and seriously lost it."

"Ah. Right," I mumbled, when what I really should be saying was you shouldn't read someone else's diary. But – *nice, polite* – I never dared speak my mind. Plus, I sort of felt sorry for old Mrs DeLacey too. "They really keep your aunt's room like a museum?"

"Yes! Even the same bed sheets!" The girl took another tissue and there was a foghorn-blow of her dainty nose. It was turning as pink as her eyes. "I only want to find out about the aunt I never got to meet! What's wrong with that?" The pretty face glared defiantly. "I'm Alice, by the way."

"Vivien."

She straightened, smoothing her sore-looking hands back over her long fair hair, like she was rearranging herself. "My mum said my aunt was looking for the Lake Mermaid." A purposeful lick of her lips. "And the diary I found was titled '*My Mermaid Diary*'. I never got the chance to read past the first page but there's a mystery. I'm sure of it. My family are hiding secrets from me about what *really* happened to my aunt!" Her eyes were completely dry now, like they were taps – on, off.

"Have you ever seen the Lake Mermaid?" she asked abruptly.

If I'd had drink in my mouth, I'd have spat it out. "Err, no, course not!" I shot out a laugh, halting immediately as Alice's eyes grew watery again.

She drew a slim arm up and pointed out of the shop window. "But you're right next to the water. And you sell mermaids! I thought if anyone could tell me more about the Lake Mermaid, this shop could."

I open-closed my mouth, soundless as a goldfish. "Um, well, yeah, but really it's just some old legend," I murmured.

"But didn't some village girls from the olden days *find* the Mermaid World?"

I shrugged kindly.

"Why would they make it up?"

I wrinkled my nose and surreptitiously gazed round our shop. The Mermaid Girls? I'd only ever thought of them as a way to sell more dolls. Though that didn't stop me quietly boasting, "My great-great-gran arrived here from Ireland, poor and alone, and the Mermaid Girls helped her start Enchanted Tails," before I admitted, "But the Lake Mermaid – it's a story for the tourists, really." *Kerching!*

Alice's perfect oval face seemed to go through a whole catalogue of expressions: confusion, surprise, indignation, till it settled on Massive Disappointment.

That one I knew. It had been spreading through me like a bushfire since yesterday afternoon.

"So now I feel stupid," she bristled, and handed me back a ball of soggy, used tissues. "You've been super nice, thank you." She jumped up and stalked a prompt catwalk to the door, Tinkerbell waving her wand as she left.

I dropped the wet tissues into the bin and sidled back to the till. I stared goggle-eyed at the mess of pert-nosed mermaids there, idly shifting them up into sitting. I gazed back at Mum's Crowning photo. I drummed my fingers on the counter and stared out at the lake. Then – without even making a proper decision in my head – I was suddenly running out of the shop in a Tinkerbell frenzy.

"Hey!" I called after the sunshine-yellow head passing Atlantis Arcades as it opened, its multicoloured mermaid lights blinking to a cacophony of piped music.

"Actually, when I think about it – " I was breathless as I reached her – "I do know a lot about mermaids." Well, I *sold* them.

"So you *can* tell me more about the Lake Mermaid?" Alice's eyes grew hopeful.

"I can!" I nodded.

"When? When can you?"

This Alice, she had a definite, determined tone to her voice – the sort that spurs you to take action *immediately*. "Erm, maybe when I finish at the shop later? I can do you a mermaid tour if you like?" I coughed to clear the overeagerness from my voice.

"And *do* you believe there might actually be a mermaid in the lake?"

Those deep-sea eyes were moving over mine like a hypnotist as if this was a dangerous game of truth or dare.

I gulped past the lump of disappointment in my throat that kept reminding me: Mum didn't think I was good enough. My answer came out croaky, but clear. "I suppose – maybe I do."

The Mermaid Girls

"One selkie jewellery box; one fabric mermaid doll; two nixie keyrings!"

I listed what I'd sold extra-brightly when Mimi arrived back at lunchtime – even if we both knew it was poor takings for a Saturday – because she really looked like she needed cheering up.

"Well, it's better than a slap in the face with a mermaid tail!" It was one of our usual jokes, but Mimi's accompanying smile looked too heavy for her mouth. There was a cat's cradle of lines on her forehead now. As if there was more to worry about than just Mum.

"Were things bad at the bank?" I trailed her as she began to rearrange the mermaid dolls on the counter. "Maybe you should stop putting money in my Future savings account."

Mimi reached towards me and cupped my cheek. "Never!" She made a frazzled dance of her head. "No, it was just the festival committee meeting – it's getting hard enough to entice tourists to choose Splendour over Spain without our young people making complaints about the Mermaid Crown to the village council."

"Complaints?" The Mighty Protestors shot into my mind and out of my mouth. I hurriedly told her what Hero had said, adding, "And Eleni wants to join the MPs! She licks Hero's feet!" It was always a relief to offload my problems on to Mimi.

Except she didn't pick up on the hurt tone of my voice.

"If our own villagers start to find fault with mermaids –" a sigh catapulted her eyes around the dolls in the shop – "then it could spell real trouble for us." She rested her gaze anxiously on the window display. "Never mind all these parade costumes to shift…"

"But no one will agree with the MPs." I hated Mimi looking weighed down and creased; it made my insides do the same. "Everyone loves the Crown and seeing Lake Splendour in the national press!" I tried to sound encouraging.

"Oh, *you*. What would I do without my Vivien?" It got me another face-cup before her hand dropped to an arm-rub, like she was making a bump better. "We're going to put your mum's cancelled visit behind us, yes? She was the same when she was little: rebellious, mischievous, never did anything she was told. Not like you, my good, clever girl."

Mimi stared at me extra-long, extra-hard, as if all her hopes for our mermaid shop rested on me being *clever* and *good*. Then she brightened with an idea. "I know, let's treat ourselves to a chippy tea later on. A selkie box, one mermaid and a couple of keyrings should cover a small battered cod each. What d'you say?"

I checked my watch. The girl, Alice, was really late. I felt like the White Rabbit waiting impatiently for its golden-haired heroine. The lake was brown-grey today – it's always changing colour. A faint swirling mist was keeping tourists off the shore: unhired rowing boats bobbed by the jetty and the ice-cream cabin had closed early. Eyes skyward: towards the two bronze heads directly above me. I'd told Alice to meet me here, at the Mermaid Girls sculpture. It's where the official tourist trail starts if you have a pound spare for a map. The village makes a right old fuss of this area, with pretty flower baskets and a bandstand where music plays on sunny days. It's also where the girls line up to get their mermaid costumes judged for the Mermaid Crown. I'd entered once myself, a few years ago. My stomach curdled at the memory. I'd overheard Charlie Tate laughing about me with his friends as I lined up to be judged: "Vivien's more Shrek than The Little Mermaid." It sort of put me off – I lowered my eyes from the sculpture, fiddling with my anorak sleeves – you know, from entering again.

"Watch it – the wind might change and leave you looking that way."

Alice DeLacey.

She pulled a face of exasperation. "That's what the battleaxe – The Dragon – is always saying." Her deep-sea blues rolled upwards.

"*Grandmothers*," I groaned dramatically for solidarity, even if Mimi wasn't anything like a battleaxe, or even officially called Grandmother.

"So tell me everything about the Lake Mermaid!" Alice said, a swing to her voice as excitable as her high ponytail – as if our mermaid was a living, local celebrity. I noticed she had eyeliner on, as well as hoop earrings. I suddenly felt a bit childish in my ancient blue anorak. I discreetly pulled out the glittery purple slide I'd added to my hair.

"OK, sooo, err, there's always been stories of a mermaid at Lake Splendour," I started, a jaggedness to my voice. There was something about Alice's direct, unwavering gaze that put me on edge, as if I might disappoint her any moment. "Long-ago fisherfolk used to call her Melusine. That's my mum's name too," I added.

Alice made a mouth-shrug.

A storyteller clear of my throat. "They used to beg Melusine for a full net and pray she wouldn't drown them. The mermaid, not my mum!"

Silence. Alice can't have realised I was joking. I took a wobbly breath. "But then, ta-da – " I extended both arms upwards dramatically to the sculpture. "The legend really took off with these two."

Alice's gaze followed mine – just as a pigeon pooed on the flowing bronze hair of one the girls.

"Sorry about that," I said, flushing as if it was me who'd done it. "Meet Lydia and Violet, who claimed they got called to the Mermaid World in nineteen fourteen."

"Claimed?" Alice said, a deep crease forming between her eyes.

I smiled uncertainly. "Well, they said the Lake Mermaid 'illuminated' them in the quarry cave." I pointed to the path that went round the water towards the Shell Grotto, then on to the Illuminated Cave. "Soon after, they both completely disappeared."

Alice's crease vanished too. It gave me a quick buzz of confidence. I wiggled my fingers spookily to keep her interest and my voice took on a ghostly tone. "Seven months they were gone, only to return at the start of the First World War. They told their families the Lake Mermaid had called them to her realm, where women and girls lead the fight for power." I grinned because I liked to tease second-best-friend Erik over that bit.

"It's why they're sculpted to look like mermaids." I pressed a hand to one bronze tail before pointing to the grey stone building the other side of the road. "Have you ever been into Lydia and Violet's old house? They lived there together before it became the village tourist office."

"Nope, never. The Dragon thinks it's all tacky." Alice was making left-right glances at Lake Splendour's promenade, as if she was trying to detect a smell in the air. "How could the Mermaid Girls possibly forsake somewhere magical to remain *here*?"

"Um, well…" I tried seeing through Alice's eyes. I suppose the flower baskets might seem a bit shabby; dreary too, with the feathery mist trailing through the grey air. I shrugged. "Maybe they missed their fish battered and wrapped in paper?"

Nope. Alice didn't seem to find that one funny either.

"But by staying they got the tourists to come and helped loads of women like my great-great-gran set up mermaid businesses," I added more solemnly as we crossed the road. "And everything changed for the girls of the village too. They got the chance to stay on at school as long as the boys. Before the war, they had to leave by fourteen – or earlier – to work in service or help out at home."

"Isn't that nice," Alice said as I held the door open for her. I couldn't tell if she was being sarcastic.

I inhaled deeply through my nose as we went inside; the tourist office smell is one of my favourites, like some familiar old teddy bear. Plus, Erik's dad is the manager and – "Ey up, chuck!" – he always has a giant grin for me.

In fact, if I got a choice in dads, I'd choose Erik's. Mum doesn't even know who mine is (except he's from a faraway country and clearly has frizzy hair. And big feet). Erik's dad has shaggy hair and a sloping smile and always wears jumpers and scarves that he knits himself all year round (you need woollies in summer here – no point pretending otherwise). Erik's mum died when she had his little sister Pearl, who's five now, so his dad does all the working and the caring, like Mimi. It's probably another reason why Erik's my second-best friend. We're both sort of lopsided when it comes to family.

"And who's this with you?" Erik's dad put down his knitting (jazzy, sparkly colours; scarf-shaped) and shared his big welcome grin with Alice, who – curling her lip – stalked away, past the postcards and fishtail pencil-toppers and holographic mermaid bookmarks, into the house.

I threw a hurried apology face at Erik's dad and chased after her, eager to explain that *he sounds like a CBeebies presenter with* everyone, *adults too*. Except Alice got there first, hissing at me, "He was *knitting*!" and "I don't trust people who are that jolly. They're hiding something."

And all right, *I know* I should have stuck up for Erik's dad who – *fact*, I'd choose as my dad – but like I told you, I really don't like to make things unpleasant.

"This used to be Lydia and Violet's kitchen," I explained instead. Now it was exhibition space for every mermaid legend going. An enthusiastic tour guide, I began pointing out the best ones. "The Zennor mermaid, she eloped with a boy from Cornwall; the mermaid's curse at Knockdolion; Sabrina, the water nymph in the River Severn. Look: Loch Meadaidh's selkie; and the malevolent mermaid who haunts Blake Mere pool.

"There're friendly mermaids too: at Bulgham Bay, and that one in the Peak District's Mermaid's Pool grants you eternal life."

I was on a roll. I began picking out the best stories from history next. "Christopher Columbus saw mermaids on his Caribbean voyage, and there's the fake Fiji mermaid that P. T. Barnum bought for his circus, and—" *Oh.* Turning round, I realised I'd been speaking to an empty room.

I found Alice in the narrow corridor, with its panels depicting Hans Christian Andersen's famous story. She was staring at the part where The Little Mermaid makes a tragic pact with the Sea Witch.

"It was her own fault," Alice said when she saw me. "Swapping a magical tail for dull land legs!"

She swept on again like she was surfing waves, into the next room: Lydia and Violet's old lounge, with its bay window overlooking the lake and framing the mountains. The exhibition panels here were all about the Mermaid Girls.

"Is that them?" Alice prodded a picture of Lydia and Violet when they were about our age, before they "met" the Lake Mermaid. "Why aren't they more beautiful?" Another sharp curl formed on her parcel-bow mouth.

"Bad photo?" I suggested. I peered in closely at the old brown and cream print, though I already knew what they looked like: ordinary. Mimi always snorted that the bronze sculpture outside was the "Disney version". Because "the tourists – they want beauty". *And what the tourists want, the tourists get.* The real Violet's cheeks were pitted with smallpox scars. She was short and stocky and had a scowl fiercer than a cornered bear. Lydia had short hair, not long like on the sculpture. Mimi said girls only cut their hair in those days if they had lice or they'd sold it for money, which meant they'd been pretty poor too, when they were young.

Alice's fingers were tapping against her arm, her head tilted like we were in some fancy art gallery. "They should look more like mermaids."

I self-consciously pulled at the tight curls at my neck and dropped a discreet glance to my Hobbit-wide feet – while Alice began reading aloud from one of the panels.

"*Lydia and Violet had to leave school at just eleven years old to help earn a living for their families. Four years later they would disappear on 16th January 1914. On their* return, they said they had been away in the Mermaid World, but that the Lake Mermaid had sent them back home to help in the Great War effort. Lydia drove ambulances in France, and Violet worked in the Lake Splendour slate quarry."

In the next picture they were older; direct stares into the camera. Lydia was dressed in her British Red Cross uniform; Violet wore a sash with the words "*Votes for Women*".

"That's a suffragette sash," I said, proud to showcase my knowledge. "I wrote an essay this term called '*Women who made a difference*' and it was all about rebellious girls and women who influenced the course of history." I hoped I was impressing her. "I included Emmeline Pankhurst – she was the leader of the suffragettes." I tried to ignore Alice's yawn. "And Lydia and Violet for changing our Lake Splendour history.

"The tourist office displayed Violet's sash once, when it was the centenary of women getting the vote!"

"What are you talking about?" Alice replied coolly.

"Erm, suffragettes – they fought for women to win the right to vote?"

"What's that got to do with mermaids?" she sniffed.

"Oh, nothing, it's just the sash shows that the Mermaid Girls were suffragettes."

Alice was still looking at me blankly.

"But the tourists are never interested in stuff like that," I moved on quickly. "They just come for the mermaid story." I tried to quickly adjust my solemn expression as Alice cast an exuberant, "Too right!"

She stepped towards the next panel and continued to read aloud: "*When the Great War ended, women had to give their jobs back to the returning soldiers.*"

She had a voice like a newsreader. I wished I could speak like that. If I spoke like that I might dare to put my hand up in class more. Maybe I'd have presented my "*Women who made a difference*" essay to the whole of my history class like Sir wanted me to and not given a fig about Charlie Tate and his mates heckling from the back row.

"*Yet, at the same time, the trenches had taken the lives of Lake Splendour miners from the slate quarries, which meant many villagers had no income,*" Alice clipped professionally. "*It was the Mermaid Girls who single-handedly saved the village and created futures for women and girls. They led a movement of tradeswomen that built the mermaid tourist trade, from hotels and tearooms to boat trips and the mermaid arts and crafts that you see today.*"

"Look, there's a picture of them opening up our shop in nineteen twenty-two!" I chipped in encouragingly, gesturing to another panel and a sepia print of Lydia and Violet cutting the ribbon in front of Enchanted Tails. Their hair was bobbed now, and both of them wore trousers.

A sharp gasp. "Lydia's only got one arm! Violet has another scar on her face, like a pirate!" Alice said, in a tone like she'd been tricked.

"War injuries," I said. "It didn't stop them making a success of the village. Enchanted Tails was the first shop for the tourists; it's passed down to the women in our family for a century." My chest was robin-puffing out. I tried not to think about tourist numbers dwindling or that I'd heard Mimi hissing into the shop phone as I left: "I told you, I've no more money to give you." It had to be the bank, or an overdue bill. I allowed myself a spit of a thought against *All-hail-Hero*: the last thing Mimi needed was complaints about the Mermaid Crown getting between the tourists and our tills.

"*Lydia survived the Great War, only to die in the Second World War, at Dunkirk in 1940,*" the posh newsreader to my right continued to read aloud from the panel. "*Violet died four years later, they say of a broken heart.*"

"Isn't it sad?" I said.

Apparently not; Alice was brightening. "Neither of them could survive here on land!" she exclaimed. "They should *never* have swapped their tails back for legs! Idiotic, like The Little Mermaid!"

I made one of Mimi's non-committal noises – "Mmmm" – rather than point out that it was a second war and heartbreak that did for Lydia and Violet. Well, I wasn't about to make Alice feel stupid, now, was I?

"*The Lake Mermaid illuminated us to new possibilities in life.*" That was me, trying some newsreading, from a panel that directly quoted Lydia on her time as a "mermaid". "*Violet and I endured a series of tests of rebellion, courage and transformation, to find a world where deeds not words mattered, where courage spreads courage, where women and girls can change their lives and seek equal power.*"

"Wow!" Alice's face lit up. *Finally I'd impressed her!* Except, no – she was shooting off across the room towards the queen conch shell in the fireplace. Spotlit there in its cabinet, on a pink velvet cushion like it was a Fabergé egg.

"It was found in the lake some five hundred years ago." Joining her, I switched back to tour guide. "Apparently, fisherfolk would hear the Lake Mermaid warning them through it: omens about perilous fogs and floods."

"It's magical." Alice pressed her palm against the glass.

"I suppose." I tried to match her enthusiasm. I mean, it's just a very old, large, pink and orange shell, hardly the Holy Grail. "The Mermaid Girls claimed –" I coughed, "*said* – that they heard the Lake Mermaid calling them through the shell."

"Really?" Alice clapped her hands. "I want to listen! Is there a key?" She shook the cabinet so hard it rattled.

"It's fragile, like over half a millennium ancient," I said quickly, to make her stop. "No one's allowed to touch it any more."

"That's not fair. We should be allowed to listen! It's our right!" Alice slammed her palm against the glass, causing it to vibrate. "Magic shells locked in cabinets: this is just another example of how the grown-ups stop our adventures!"

I took a fast breath – she had a way of saying things like she was on stage.

"You know, my mother would lock *me* in a cushioned cabinet if she could. She wants to clip my wings! That's why I've been dumped here with The Dragon for the summer!" Her blue eyes seemed to come ablaze under the bright strobe lights. "Both my parents think I'm worthless. Do you know how that feels?"

"I do," I replied earnestly.

She flashed me a wide-eyed smile. "I knew it! I knew

I saw a kindred spirit in you."

My face flushed bright pink.

"What have yours done to you?"

"Erm, well, it's just my mum." I pressed the tips of my fingers to the glass cabinet and tried to add casually, "She was supposed to be visiting me, but she cancelled last minute. She thinks Lake Splendour is dull." I licked my lips, sensing my mouth filling with a sudden confession. I really wanted to prove to Alice I *was* kindred spirit material. "I – I reckon maybe she thinks I'm dull too. Like, not exciting enough. I wanted her to visit so much."

When I looked up, the blaze behind Alice's eyes seemed to be weaving spells, light reflecting off them and making them sparkle like the lake in rare Splendour sunshine.

"So reinvent yourself to tempt her here. I reinvent myself all the time. Last year I was into vintage clothes, and this year I'm contemporary." She raised her arms stiffly above her head like a mannequin then dropped them down, latching her hands to my shoulders like claws. "If you like, I can help you: make your mum think you *are* exciting, *worth* visiting."

Her wide eyes bored into mine. "In fact, we could help each other. Like the Mermaid Girls. What do you think – is it a deal?"

I was nodding furiously before I even knew what the deal was. "Do you want help with your parents too?"

"Oh no," she said breezily, bending to stare at the conch shell again. "I've given up on mine; I despise them. No, The Dragon locked Aunt Stella's room when she found me in it. I must uncover what really happened to my aunt and her search for the Lake Mermaid."

She straightened up; that direct gaze.

"I have to read her Mermaid Diary. And you can help me steal it."

The Tail of
Lake Splendour

"Now you've made me feel stupid a second time," Alice said stiffly.

That was the last thing I wanted to do! But the look on my face must have given me away. I could never read someone's diary, never mind break into a dead girl's room and steal one!

"Forget I mentioned it." Alice was off again, back towards the main door, sending evils at Erik's dad's clickety-clack knitting needles.

"How about we go to Atlantis Arcades?" I said, joining her outside. I bent to pick up a discarded Coke can. "I can show you how to win at the penny drop; there's a special way of dropping your coin so— Hey!"

She'd flicked my hand so I dropped the can. "Ewww, germs! What are you doing?"

I started to babble about littering and our water birds, but she was cutting across me again. "Show me where the Mermaid Girls disappeared."

We got behind a straggly line of damp-looking tourists following the wooden shell-shaped sign: *This way to mermaid magic!* Through the dark tunnel carved from jagged quarry rock, water drip-dripping from the ceiling. On into the Shell Grotto, named for our celebrated queen conch shell.

A couple of tourists were gathered like bird-watchers at the grotto's wide-open window over the lake, phone cameras at the ready to catch a flash of sparkly tail. *As if.*

I watched Alice gaze round the grotto walls that were plastered with every kind of shell, ordinary and exotic: cones and clams; cowries and conches; sundials, strombus, scallops, spindles; tritons, turbos, turritellas. "You've really never been here before?"

"The Dragon won't even utter the word *mermaid*. She never usually lets me visit when there's a festival," she said, idly passing the shell-covered Mermaid Throne where a small girl, tiara, fishtail, sat being crowned for her dad's photo. We stopped at the trickling fountain dug into one wall and boasting a Lake Mermaid stone statue, erect and regal in a pool of water, carpeted with coins the tourists throw in to make a wish.

I watched Alice dig into her jeans pocket and chuck in a – *two pound!* – coin. She closed her eyes, so I closed mine too (two pounds = two wishes, surely): *Please make Mum visit soon* (even if I didn't believe in magic).

When I snapped mine open, Alice was staring at me impatiently. "Illuminated Cave?"

We circled higher, along the dug-out path that used to be a track in Victorian times for the narrow-gauge quarry train that trundled the slate from the mines to the village. The wood to our right was protected by a barbed-wire fence, preventing anyone messing around near the quarry walls and caves. I pointed between trees swollen with summer leaf. "You can sometimes spot one of our Lake Splendour red squirrels, almost as elusive as the Lake Mermaid!" I said top-gear enthusiastically – because Alice wasn't looking mightily enthralled; less so when she glimpsed the fat white bulbs strung across the entrance to the Illuminated Cave.

"They're because Lydia and Violet said they became '*illuminated*' to join the Lake Mermaid," I explained. I suppose maybe they did look a little pathetic.

"Poor person's Madame Tussaud's or what?" Alice clipped as she stepped into the gloom of the cave to meet Lake Splendour's ten life-sized mermaids.

I made a nervous laugh. The waxworks used to be my favourite part.

"The mirror's there because of the Mermaid Girls' talk of 'transformation'," I got in first, before she could criticise the large, chipped gilt-framed mirror propped up against the cave wall.

We drew up together in front of the glass. And I found myself wondering what it must be like to have Alice's reflection – *how* much easier life would be – when the Lake Mermaid joined us.

Alice yelped.

"Sorry, I should've warned you," I said hurriedly. "It's a hologram of our magical lake creature." I bobbed my head around to catch the long dark hair and fishtail again. "She only appears from a certain angle. You're supposed to '*call her to you*'." I made finger marks in the air. "It used to freak me out when I was little." In fact

– *shiver* – it still did a bit now. "Arcade penny drops?" I suggested hopefully.

Alice's bow mouth was pinched. "But how did Lydia and Violet *find* the Mermaid World?"

"Oh, through that gap in the rock over there," I pointed, stopping myself from adding *allegedly*, like a police detective. Because, if it wasn't clear before, Alice was taking this mermaid business pretty seriously. I followed her to the furthest point of the cave, the mouth in the rock that was once the main entrance to the slate mines; now covered in bars and mostly filled with stone.

"Why is it not still open?"

"The old quarry mines are dangerous – crumbling, caving in, *literally*," I said. "That's why there's barbed wire surrounding the woods too – to stop anyone exploring." Yup, other schools get train-track videos; we get educational films about the dangers of rockfalls and having fatal cave adventures.

"You're saying that's it? No one can ever reach the Mermaid World again?" Alice bit out.

"Well, erm, it's just, I suppose they don't want anyone getting hurt searching for mermaids." I went insta-red the moment the words left my mouth – wasn't that how her aunt died?

Maybe that's why Alice suddenly decided she had to

53

get back home.

Stupid. I could kick myself. Three times I'd upset her now – and I really wanted Alice to like me. Being with her this afternoon was making that Mum-shaped lump in my throat shrink temporarily to frozen pea.

As we rejoined the promenade, I tried one last time to impress her with my knowledge. "Did you know – a lake is dying from the moment it's created?" I cast a theatrical arm across the water that was reflecting an upside-down world from the hills either side. "Which means one day all its mermaid secrets will be revealed."

Alice shook her head furiously. "I don't like waiting. I hate secrets!" She stopped dead in her tracks, reaching out claw-like again, her shredded, red-sore fingers latching on to my anoraked arm. "Don't you *want* to find out if the Lake Mermaid exists?

"Those Mermaid Girls had each other. I just wish I had someone to support me." A watery blink. She did seem to cry easily; maybe it was our hard northern air. "Someone to help steal my aunt's Mermaid Diary from under The Dragon's beady eye."

Oh no, not dead-girl's-diary again.

"A Watson to my Holmes. Someone excellent at sneaking and spying," she continued, flashing me a full-teeth smile as if she was already looking at the perfect person for the job. She *really* didn't know me. Subterfuge, disguise, pretence; I pulled a face of apology. I'd be hopeless.

"Don't you ever do things you're not supposed to?"

Nervous laugh. "Sure, yeah." *Absolutely not.* Apart from, maybe, sneaking a look at my phone after bedtime or stealing biscuits from the jar.

"Something mysterious happened to Stella, I know it." Alice started walking away, backwards. "I have to find out what The Dragon is hiding from me."

"Hello, love." Mimi smiled as Tinkerbell announced me. "What you been up to?"

"I told you." I peered out of the shop window, watching Alice disappear from view, up the road to the big la-di-da houses. I'd never even got her number. "I was meeting Alice DeLacey." I *knew* Mimi hadn't been listening when I left. I started straightening a disorderly shelf of water sprites with sniggering faces.

"Alice DeLacey?" Mimi said. "Oh no, love, you can't be making friends with her."

I glanced around; Mimi's bright expression had fallen like a veil from her face. "The DeLaceys are strange folk. They wouldn't want their granddaughter hanging around with you."

With me? I froze, water sprite grinning in my hand.

"Sweetheart, it's just, we're not their sort of people. You're a village girl," she said, like we were in some fairy tale and Alice was a prince, me the pauper.

"Now, what d'you say: is it time for our cod dinner?" Mimi went across to our ancient brass till and thumped it, its cash drawer cranking open to reveal the day's paltry notes and card receipts. She slid out a twenty-pound note, thrusting it towards me with another weighty smile that seemed to cover up a not-smile. "My good, clever girl," she said.

My insides started throbbing like I'd plunged into ice-cold water.

Good. Clever. Not beautiful. Never exciting.

I was stomping, not walking, to Poseidon. Mum didn't think I was worth visiting. Mimi didn't think I was *worthy* of Alice. *Alice was too sophisticated, too pretty, too posh for the likes of me!*

Faster stomps; fingers of mist like shredded string travelling with me, making the air wetter, colder, its moisture shrinking my hair into even tighter curls. Past Nature's Bounty – today's mermaid showcase a fuzzy pear on top of a scaly pineapple – and on into our village shopping precinct, past Musical Scales and Dive into Books before – deep-breath-salt-and-vinegar – I joined the end of the chip-shop queue. On to tiptoes to exchange a wave with Eleni, working hard alongside her parents; sometimes I helped out too for extra money. By the time I reached the counter I was desperate to tell Eleni everything, about Alice and secret dead-girl diaries and Mum not coming and…

"Where shall I put the haddock?" *All-hail-Hero* was emerging from the back with a tray of floured fish.

"I meant to call you to see if you were free to help," Eleni said in a rush, clocking my face.

At the same time my eyes spotted her shop apron: a badge there, emblazoned with four rainbow-coloured words: *STOP the Mermaid Crown!*

My mouth seemed to freeze and I could only just mumble my order; eyes pinned to the floor where my heart and stomach lay splayed beside my feet. It was clear: Eleni did not care one jot that supporting anti-mermaid fever might spell the end of Enchanted Tails. I didn't ask for extra vinegar as she wrapped it up.

Sulkier stomps back towards the lake – the wisps of fog transforming from string to rope now – weaving past old people taking their evening constitutionals. "That's how I want my perm, Enid." I looked round: *yes*, the two old women were pointing at me.

Mimi's good girl. I imitated the words silently. *And where's good got me?* Mum had her exciting cruise ships; clearly, Eleni had *Hero*. What did I have? Besides shrinking hair and massive feet?

The humongous lump was back, swollen with a vengeance in my throat. Even the delicious warm waft of my dinner couldn't placate me. I passed a promenade bin with day-tripper rubbish overspilling on to the pavement and a burst of exasperation exploded across my chest. I could still hear Alice saying, *Don't you ever do anything you shouldn't?* as I abruptly turned into Atlantis Arcades. I *could* be mischievous – with Mimi's chippy change. I walked past the owner, Ursula Undine (self-named), lodged like a frog on a lily pad in her glass change cabin and glaring at every customer like they'd cheated. On past the penny drops, heading instinctively for my favourite: Mermaid Messenger. An ancient arcade game from the Lydia and Violet days that no one else seemed to play but me. All gilt metal and giant lever with an eyepiece to a mermaid who sparkles across the viewfinder and dispenses a written message each time. When I was little I used to pretend the messages were from my mum, and keep them all in a shoebox like you might save voicemails on your phone.

Ten pence in the slot and I yanked on the lever. The

mermaid danced then disappeared. Click. Clunk. The machine spat out its message.

Don't fear flying too fast; be scared of standing still.

Sure, right. I shoved it into my anorak pocket. I'd stopped keeping them in a shoebox years ago.

Trudging back outside, a heron was skimming the mist above the lake, grazing the waves before stretching out its long, graceful wings to ascend again. It made me think of Mum, my stork: "*Delivered you; took off.*" Because the world of Lake Splendour was too small for her. Our craggy mountains in the distance suddenly took on the shape of a sleeping giant, holding me captive. *Cages across caves; conch shell locked in a cabinet.*

I retrieved my mermaid message from my pocket. *Don't fear flying too fast; be scared of standing still.* And I resumed walking. *Fast.* On past our shop (even though our battered fish wanted putting on plates). Past the sign *Welcome to Lake Splendour* and up the road, rising above the water, alongside evergreens like cathedral spires, keeping the few big houses up here private and secluded and silent. I rarely came up this hill. If I did it was in the car, never on foot. The glimpses of lake between the trees appeared magical, a silky canopy of mist hovering above it, like some private paradise.

Panting with the fast ascent, I soon reached the

DeLacey house – at the top of the road before it circled off from the lake and into the mountains. Its wrought-iron gates were closed. I peered through them like a prisoner, at the striped fake-Tudor building at the end of a massive gravel driveway. I knew the DeLacey house was dead posh – I could see that when I rowed on the lake – but up close it was even grander, a palace almost.

I straightened my old blue anorak and patted down my rain-sprung hair before I reached for the buzzer on the stone plinth and – bottled it. Shoulders slumping, I turned away.

Whoosh.

A pair of tanned legs shot into my peripheral vision, stretching out long and lean and bronze against the mournful sky.

Vanished again.

I shifted my gaze back between the iron bars.

Alice. Soaring through the sky. Her hands clutching the rope of a tyre swing tied to a broad oak tree. Her straight glossy hair rising and falling like a veil of sunshine behind her.

"Alice!' I called, waving, jumping, so she'd see me behind the gates. Something with wings was stirring inside of me. "It's a deal. I'll be your Watson!"

Erik The Viking

"What, you mean Lake Splendour's mermaid?"

"Are there others?" I made a joke-face at Erik. We were waiting, last in line as usual, at Monday's holiday swim club at the pool.

"So *do* you think it's possible that the Lake Mermaid could –" I paused. I might as well have been asking if there's a Gruffalo in the woods – "could actually live in the lake?"

"Anything's possible, Vivien!"

This is why Erik is my second-best friend. Erik never makes me feel daft or odd. And he always looks on the bright side, whatever life throws at him.

Like he always shrugs off any mean comments he gets about the way he looks (he gets a fair bit, what with his being a little on the wider side and a fan of his dad's home-knitted range).

Like he never complains about coming from a lopsided family: he sends his dad a card on Mother's and Father's Days.

Like he never seems to care that we're always – and I mean, *always* – pushed to last in line at swim club (even if we're first to leave the changing room).

I bet Alice DeLacey would never allow herself to get pushed to last, I decided, staring down the queue to watch Jonty, our swim instructor, demonstrate the forward pike dive he wanted us to try. *I'm-so-cool* Charlie Tate was first up (*course*), followed by Princess Table's Sahana and Lily. Their (straight) hair was tied up in neat topknots, not wedged under a tight swim cap like mine (that always left a red lobotomy line on my forehead). All three of them were standing straight, chins raised. It was only as you moved further down the line that shoulders started to slouch. By the time you got to Erik and me, we were almost hunched over, our arms wrapped like strangleweed round our bodies. Erik often admitted to feeling self-conscious in only his trunks. Just lately, I'd started to feel that a bit too, the way my body was changing; bumpier and hairier.

"What about the queen conch shell?" I asked Erik as we watched Charlie Tate climb the ladder to the diving board. "Didn't you say your dad once let you listen to it?"

"Yeah, when I was little. I wanted to pass Mum a message through it, after she died. I swear I heard a voice come out!"

"You're joking? You've never told me that!" I felt a tingling inside. What if Alice *was* right to believe in the Lake Mermaid?

"It was well creepy," he grinned. See, Bright-Side Erik.

Charlie hit the water. His dive was pretty rubbish. But, lo and behold, nearly the whole of swim club applauded him like he'd just won Olympic Gold.

"Do you think your dad might let me have a listen?" I said, already picturing Alice's face lit up with appreciation (*Wow, you're amazing, Vivien!*).

Except Erik creased his face for "sorry".

I exhaled glumly. "If only the Lake Mermaid *was* real,

then we'd get tons more tourists."

"You're right there. Dad says visitors are well down from last summer. We've got a surplus of postcards."

And *yes*, we did sound like two old people waiting at the bus stop. Erik and I sort of had that effect on each other.

"Did you know the Mighty Protestors have complained about mermaids to the village council?" I added, relieved to get more off my chest. Though I wasn't expecting Erik's eyes to go so wide.

"So that's what they were arguing about at Saturday's committee meeting! I was at the tourist office stock-counting the mermaid-tail pencil-toppers: they're still our bestseller, you know, that and—"

I made a noise to get him to his point.

"Sorry. Yeah, your gran, my dad, the rest of the committee – they were talking about *sabotage*! A threat's been made: stop the Mermaid Crown or risk the whole festival getting ruined!" Erik's reassuring smile at the end didn't quite match his words.

I narrowed my eyes on the chlorine-blue pool water, picturing Eleni's pin-badge with *STOP the Mermaid Crown!* and Mimi looking worried. "The Mighty Protestors are just troublemakers!"

"The committee sounded in a right ole pickle." Erik

made a sigh like an old farmer. "Deirdre from Conch Curios was talking all hush-hush about what if the protestors dig around and find out the truth about the Mermaid Girls. Some secret about Lydia and Violet being imprisoned."

"*Imprisoned?*"

"Think so. I didn't hear the rest cos I had to see to our Pearl. She was displaying the mermaid bookmarks *all* wrong."

"Someone needs to stop the MPs." I interrupted him with a hot puff of air from my mouth. "If only the Lake Mermaid *was* real."

"Be careful what you wish for, Vivien!" Erik laughed, then grew abruptly solemn. "But, about the Mermaid Crown—" He kept his mouth open to say more, then stopped.

"What is it?" I nudged him. Erik hardly ever wore a frown.

"Ahh, nowt," he answered, skating his bare foot across a tile puddle. "We just need the Crown."

"Exactly, and what's wrong with stopping littering instead?" I added.

"Baffles me," Erik said, snapping back to his cheery self. He leaned forward, gazing softly at someone down the line. "Do you think I should add a somersault to my pike dive when it's my turn?"

"No!" I replied quickly – because I already knew what had prompted that thought: Erik's ill-fated mission to impress perfect Sahana.

"Just do what Jonty wants," I added firmly. I couldn't bear the thought of Erik being laughed about on the Princess Table.

Erik made a dejected nod and now we both wiggled our wide feet in tile puddles, waiting while everyone else took their turn to dive. I tried not to think about the MPs, or about Eleni caring more for Hero than about Enchanted Tails going bust. It made pins and needles strike out all over my stomach. Instead, I let myself return to Alice soaring on her tyre swing on Saturday. Something about Alice made me feel like I could lift off and fly too. When I'd got home that night (luckily Mimi was still too preoccupied to notice cold chips), I'd even had the courage to boldly draft a message to Mum: Can't you come see me in the festival Lake Race?

I'd not sent it, of course. I took a steadying breath of warm-chemical air. Because what if she said no? Still, it was a start, right?

"Earth calling Erik and Vivien!"

We both glanced up at Jonty's voice. And – *great* – now the whole line was staring our way. I re-gripped my exposed body parts.

"Yo, Earth calling the aliens!" Charlie Tate was repeating in a nasty voice, as Erik and I began our wet walk slap-slapping to the diving board together. Because, despite the width of my feet, I'm prone to slipping and Erik always grabs me if I feel myself going.

"Look, he's wobbling like jelly! Watch out for the tsunami!" Charlie again. Some of the others laughed.

"Ignore him," I whispered to Erik. In another life, I imagined myself the sort of person who'd turn round and bop Charlie one on the nose. Instead, I just sent my second-best friend a thumbs-up as he climbed the ladder first.

Now, you might not think it to look at Erik, but he dives like a gannet and swims like a water-snake. A commander of water like some conquering Viking. Yeah, I hear others talk about him: *How can he be one of the fastest swimmers in the village?* Well, they should look past his round, soft stomach. Erik's more of a miracle than any lake mermaid. "It's all in the technique," Erik teases. But I don't think even he knows exactly what his magic is. Maybe some people are just born to live in water, not on land.

Except – get this – hardly anyone applauded for Erik's dive (which was magnificent, by the way; the best of the boys for sure). Just me, and Jonty, and a couple of others. *It's not fair*, I told my Hobbit feet as I made my ascent to the diving board. I tried to block out the Charlie-whispers travelling up with me, "Looks like an egghead in that swim cap", "It's cos her electrified hair can't touch water. *Zizzzzz*". Instead I held fast on to Alice, soaring on that swing; to making Mum proud if she came to watch me in the Lake Race after all. Hands in an arrow, chin tucking into my chest, and – down – I headed towards the cold chlorine-blue. *Whoosh*, my knotted stomach fled my body. For just a few seconds there, I was no longer Ordinary Village Girl, frizzy-haired Vivien – *splash* – I was the closest I'd ever get to being a mermaid.

Erik and I were leaving the leisure centre, heading for our usual post-swim hot chocolate at Splash Tearooms. Erik was describing what he'd do to get his own back on Charlie Tate if he ever had the courage. "I'd shove him and his gob right into the pool."

"Or you could win Neptune's trident this year – that'd show him!"

Erik's reply was unusually jittery. "Actually, I was thinking of entering the Mermaid Crown – maybe."

I halted, dread for my friend snaking my stomach.

"It's just, I think it's more me than Neptune." He smiled weakly, fumbling through his rucksack and tugging at some material that looked holographic shiny and – fishy. "Dad's helping me make a showstopper of a costume."

"Ah, Erik, I'm not sure…" I was groping for the kindest words to make him see it was a bad idea – *bad, Erik!* – that Charlie Tate would eat him for dinner, when I spotted her.

Alice. Leaning against the wall beside a mermaid-bin like she was posing for an album cover. I'd told her about swim club; she must have looked up the times. The thought gave my stomach another diving-board leap. Quick smooth down of dishevelled hair; a rub at the red lobotomy line on my forehead. I couldn't help a smile when I noticed Sahana and Lily appraising Alice as they passed – Alice's jacket looked expensive; trainers the latest Nikes; hair silkier than any on the Princess Table.

And she was my new friend.

"Good news!" Alice bounced on her heels as she saw me. "The Dragon's going to the garden centre soon. Commence *Operation Mermaid Diary!*" she announced, sending a quick suspicious glance at a grinning Erik next to me.

"Oh – sorry – yeah, this is Erik," I introduced him.

"What's *Operation Mermaid Diary* then?" Erik said cheerfully, knotting his – dad-knitted – sparkly scarf around his neck.

Alice's instant expression was, shall we say, less cheerful. I jumped in. "Erik's listened to the queen conch shell!" I knew if Alice got to know Erik, she'd love him too; she'd see how funny and kind he was. "He even heard a voice once!" I added excitedly.

Alice assessed Erik coolly. "*You* heard the Lake Mermaid?"

"Hmm, I dunno if that's who it was." Erik seemed to be wilting under Alice's direct stare; two bright-pink spots had appeared on his round face. "I hope not," he laughed. "Rumour has it she lures fishermen to their death."

I nudged Erik to shush, though he wasn't to know that the girl who died twenty years ago searching for mermaids was Alice's aunt.

A dramatic hair-flip and Alice turned her back on Erik. "Come on, Vivien, we have to go, *now*. The Dragon's hardly ever out." She gave me one of her glorious smiles and looped her arm through mine like she was propelling me to first in line.

"Aren't we going for hot chocolate?" Erik broke in.

The pink spots were expanding.

"Um, oh yeah," I faltered. "Alice, you want to come with me and Erik to Splash Tearooms first?"

"But, *Viv*?" She shortened my name. No one did that, except Mum. My stomach flipped and lifted off. "This is super important, you know that!" Her eyes were watery again.

I wavered for a moment – two sets of eyes on me, one set jolly, one insistent (and a bit wet). I took a short breath. "D'you mind if we do it another time, Erik?"

Alice needed me.

OK – *fine* – I needed Alice.

The Land
of Giants

This time the wrought-iron gates were wide open and I got to walk across the crunching gravel driveway and up to the grand, mock-Tudor front door. I tried to scrape off any dirt from my trainers before I followed Alice inside. I caught my breath – whoa, their hallway was massive, the size of our entire flat. Like something from a magazine spread. It even had a gong – a gong! – as if there was no way you could shout anyone for dinner in a house this size. I thought of our tiny hallway, stacked high with boxes of dolls, and I silently vowed never to take Alice home.

"OK, you stand guard here," Alice commanded, "while I go and search The Dragon's bedroom for the key. The Sleeping Grandpa will be in his deckchair. Sound the gong if the monster returns." And she was off, bounding up the grand wooden staircase before I could even say, *Can't I come too?*

Not that I really wanted to go rooting through old-lady lingerie. I just didn't want to be left alone down here either.

Take your job seriously, I tried telling myself. *Alice trusts you.* The pep talk worked for about two seconds before my palms started to feel damp. Somewhere a clock seemed to tick more loudly; my heartbeats started to compete with it. I was suddenly in the middle of a huge bank robbery – me, the getaway driver.

I let out a breath of relief when Alice reappeared at the top of the staircase. She was flicking through a wad of cash in her hand as she descended. *Was* it a bank robbery? A glance my way, as if she'd forgotten I was there. "The key's not in her old-lady-stink-bomb bedroom." She stuffed the money into her jacket pocket.

It was making me more nervous; I wanted to leave

now. "We could go and rent a boat on the lake? That's the best way to look for mermaids!" I tried to sound Erik-cheerful, when there was a noise of a car engine outside.

Alice rushed towards a side window. "Eurgh, The Dragon's back already." She seemed more peeved than perturbed.

We both ducked down as a grey head marched by, fiercely crunching gravel around the side of the house.

"You'll have to go into the garden and keep her busy while I finish looking."

"Me?" Jonty might as well have asked me to parade in my swimsuit at school assembly. "I can't do that." Really. I couldn't.

"But you said you'd help." Alice made a capital O of her mouth. "We have to find the diary!"

Yeah, I'll admit, I did like the emphasis on "we", but: "I'll be no good," I confessed. I was rubbish at faking, I could never lie without going bright pink, and then there was what Mimi had said: Mrs DeLacey wouldn't want Alice being friends with an ordinary village girl.

"You'll be ace, brilliant, the best!" She gave me a little push. "Ask her about her roses. She loves those pathetic flowers more than me! Go on.

"Go fight The Dragon for me, Viv!"

"Fight The Dragon," I repeated to myself as I numbly followed its fiery path across the driveway; fairy steps so the gravel didn't crunch and warn it of my approach.

Ace, brilliant, the best – was that really how Alice saw me? It sent a bolt of courage through me, until I saw the garden behind the house: the size of a field. That lawn went on forever, looming over the lake, the promenade below in miniature. I was one of Gulliver's giants up here, looking down on Lake Splendour's Lilliputians. I could put our shop in between my finger and thumb.

My stomach gave a greedy twitch. If we had this much money we'd never have to worry about declining tourists or dwindling sales of smug mermaids. I could do away with my old anorak, get the same phone as everyone else.

I forced myself on towards where old Mrs DeLacey was kneeling, prodding soil in a rose border with fierce jabbing movements. Grey-white hair bound in a neat bun at her neck. Nearby, an old man was snoring in a striped deckchair, folded blue cloth for a blanket.

I held my hands together neatly and murmured an adult-polite, "Hello there," trying to keep the rapid heartbeats out of my voice.

A glance as sharp as her soil-jabbing. "Who are you

and why have you got a pink line on your forehead?"

Hers was pale and rice-papery thin above piercing dots for eyes.

"Ahhh. Yeah." I touched my head. "I have to wear a swim cap because I can't get my hair wet, and the thing is…" I ramble when I'm nervous. "It's just – it doesn't get on with hairdryers, or water, or damp air, but—"

"What *are* you talking about?" Her voice was a dog-bark. "I said, who are you?" She straightened up, holding a bunch of blue and yellow roses in her arm like she was the Queen of Hearts. Tall for an old woman, with an iron-rod back.

"If you're looking for the lake waterfall, turn around. It's on our private land; we own it!"

"You do? Erm, no, I'm Vivien." My voice trembled. I was no dragon fighter. Fiery, scaly things.

"And why?" she said, dancing her garden fork.

"Err, well, my gran chose it, after Vivien, the Lady of the Lake –" let rambling recommence – "Vivien appears in Arthurian legend as Merlin's partner. She was so powerful, she entrapped him." Older people usually like that story. They ooh and ahh and tell me, *My, what a lovely name*, and some even start to recite some Walter Scott poem about another Lady of the Lake.

Nope. Not this old person.

76

"What?" Impatient bark, looking at me as though I was thoroughly mad, an eye to my forehead again, as if: *This girl* does *have trouble with her brain.* "I'm asking *why* are you here? I don't want to know about the origin of your name!" she added, admittedly with a laugh, but the kind that made me wish I did have armour and a shield.

I sniffed my shoulder. Maybe I smelled of "village girl". A glance down at my old anorak, and oh, I'd forgotten I was wearing my third-worst joggers and my no-brand trainers Mimi got from the charity shop. Everything I owned was second-hand. I still slept in Mum's old bed from when she was little.

"Where on earth is Alice?" The Dragon started to move past me.

"Wait!" I spluttered. I was going to fail my new friend. She'd see I wasn't ace, or brilliant, nowhere near best! "What unusual roses!" I tried my hardest to fake that posh newsreader voice of Alice's. "What type are they?" An expression on my face like one of those TV gardening presenters Mimi watches (even though all we've got are two window boxes).

Old Mrs DeLacey paused. She gazed down lovingly at the bouquet in her arms. "Aren't they exquisite?" Her tone seemed to lose its abruptness. "The canary-yellow is a mermaid rose. The lavender-blue is one I've created myself: the Stella rose." She bent towards the blue petals and inhaled really deeply, like she was trying to get more than an aroma.

I swallowed before I said, "After your younger daughter?"

The Dragon's head tilted suspiciously. "Are you from Lake Splendour, Vivien?"

"Uh-huh," I confessed. *Hello, village girl here.* "My gran, Mimi, runs Enchanted Tails." I tried to say it grandly, like it was Marks & Spencer and Mimi was some big CEO, and I was – no way – just any *ordinary* village girl.

She saw straight through it. Her jaw did this strange movement as if her bottom teeth had dislodged.

"It's a shop that sells—"

"Yes, yes, I know very well what it sells," she cut through me. "And I don't mean to be blunt, but I think it's time you went back there."

Tricking
The Dragon

My size sevens hadn't budged. I'd never been told to leave anywhere – well, except that time in geography when Eleni and I got the giggles because we spotted a place called Brokenwind. I stared at the ground, a sudden affinity with the shrivelled petals there.

"I'm sorry if I sound rude," The Dragon said in a voice that sounded anything but sorry, "but I think it's for the best if you don't come here again, Vivien."

Mimi had been right: I wasn't good enough for Alice. I didn't belong in the land of giants.

I was chewing hard on my bottom lip. I wanted to stick up for myself, like Alice did, like the girls I researched for my "*Women who made a difference*" essay last term.

Argue back at this straight-backed old woman and her papery-thin skin that, *actually*, I was one of the best swimmers in my school! And my *mum* travelled the world on luxury cruise ships! Enchanted Tails – *I'll have you know* – was the first mermaid shop opened in Lake Splendour!

Instead, I got saved.

"Making Viv feel welcome, are we, Grandmother?" Alice. "Playing nicely?"

Whoa there. I'd never dare use that tone of voice on Mimi.

"It's OK, I'll just go," I interjected. I didn't want to cause any trouble. I started to slip away, across the lawn, on to the driveway, heavy gravel-crunching this time, eyes blinky. *Don't cry, not till you're home.*

"Keep your hair on, old woman!" I could hear Alice shouting. Soon after, she was coming up behind me. A dramatic wink of her eye. "Changing of the guards!" And she pushed something cold and metal into my hand.

"You found the key," I said weakly, my mind struggling

to understand why she'd given it to me.

"I'll keep her with those blasted roses."

That's why.

Alice was already pushing me back through the front door of the house, her blue eyes boring into mine, as if we were telepathic. "First-floor landing. Take a right, end of the corridor, last door. The diary is in the top drawer of the bedside cabinet. Be quick."

It must have been my fierce head-shaking that made her add, "You want your mum to think you're exciting, don't you?"

And then the door closed and she was gone. And I was alone again in the massive magazine-spread hallway with the ominous tick-tock of some distant clock.

Alice wanted *me* to steal a dead girl's diary?

Heart beating faster than the clock this time, I started to climb the wide staircase – like it was the tallest diving board in the world. I was trying not to hear what Mimi would say if she knew what I was up to (*"my good, clever girl"*). I tried instead to hear Mum, telling me once (with a dramatic toss of her hair), "When I was your age, Viv, I was daring."

I pressed my palm tightly around the key: *take a right*, along a thick, soft carpet, my mouth turning dry, bones stiffening with dread; *end of the corridor* – to –

huge gulp – Alice's dead aunt's bedroom. My key hand was trembling. *You don't break into locked bedrooms*, a voice that was part mine, part Mimi's began a lecture in my head. *You don't go behind old ladies' backs*. The voice was right – I mean, I still felt bad for giggling about Brokenwind in geography. I let out a deep breath of surrender: I'd never be daring like Alice and Mum. I began softly retracing my steps, as my phone buzzed in my jacket pocket. I was hoping it was a message from Alice, telling me to call it off, *step away from the crime scene*, then she'd never have to know I wimped out.

It was *All-hail-Hero* on the screen. Eleni had forwarded a video.

"*Are you sick and tired of mermaids?*" Hero was shouting. "*Join the fight this Thursday to stop the Mermaid Crown!*"

A spool of wire wool in my stomach started knitting faster than Erik's dad's needles as I read Eleni's message below: Vivien, won't you just come along and hear why mermaids are wrong?

I wasn't sure what was worse: that the MPs' evil sabotage was definitely going ahead or the fact Eleni was inviting me to *join in* – when Enchanted Tails was at stake!

The key in my palm suddenly seemed to come to life.

I swiftly returned to the door, unlocked it and stepped inside before I had a chance to change my mind.

Flip. Stella DeLacey really did dig mermaids. The proof was everywhere: mermaid dolls, mermaid cushions, mermaid lampshade. Alice was right too about it being a museum. Everything, from its posters to the purple satin bedcover, looked really dated; even the air smelled old. I remembered Erik saying he sometimes slept with his mum's cardigan – and I sort of got it, why Mrs DeLacey might not want to change anything.

I edged forwards, immediately spying myself in the mirrored wardrobe doors to my left – like one of the bears creeping in on Goldilocks: broad-shouldered, frizzy-haired … and a criminal to boot. It forced me into a faster dash, around purple satin to the bedside cabinet; quick pull on the top drawer.

It was there, like Alice said. A 2001 diary with a picture of an underwater scene and the words *"My Mermaid Diary"* written across the front in red pen. I gently lifted it out, catching sight of something bright and green glinting beneath. I reached for that too: a hexagonal-shaped jewel; glass-like, beautiful. It felt almost powerful in my hand, like it was tempting me to steal it along with the diary. I held it up to the light and it reflected me back, in miniature, green … almost magical. Ominous

Clock made a series of loud dongs. I threw the jewel back in the drawer and shoved the diary in my swim bag.

Seconds later I was flying back out through the front door heading towards the iron gates, not daring to look around, until: abrupt stop. *Nooo* – the gates were closed again. I glanced back towards the house, a surge of panic sprouting wings up my windpipe. How would I explain why I was still here? What if Alice's gran searched me and discovered her dead daughter's diary?!

"Go!"

Alice again, shooting round the side of the house, her slim legs pistons, cheeks pink, smile wide – like this was all just fun – while her grandmother called for her. "Alice! Come back here, young lady!"

The Alice who was now hurtling past me. "Quick, climb over!" she said as she began scaling the gates like she was some soldier in training.

I could hear the crunch of Dragon-marching feet. My heart became a bomb in my chest. I rushed to climb like Alice, except not like Alice. The spikes at the top of the gate pierced my hands painfully, stinging my skin like it was on fire. I flung myself clumsily on to the ground the other side.

"Run!" Alice said in a laughing shout. "Fast!" And, limping a little, I sped after her down the road.

Alice was whooping a battle cry, like we really had just slayed a fierce dragon. "That was exhilarating!" She reached her hands towards the trees to high-five their branches.

I tried to laugh and whoop too, to not think of Mrs DeLacey chasing us like we were naughty Peter Rabbits escaping Mr McGregor.

Feet slapping concrete, we reached the lakeside, breathless.

"I suppose I could've just pressed the button to open the gates," Alice grinned. Her hands were still raised in the air, like she was travelling on some fast fairground ride.

I returned a nervous laugh. "What? Why didn't you?"

"Because it was more fun to climb the gates and break out, stupid!" A sudden leap and she grabbed my bruised hands and she began to spin us both round, making me dizzy, taking me on the fairground ride with her.

Then she pulled me into a hug, as if we'd been friends for years, not days, and I could feel her heart beating excitedly against mine.

And I suddenly realised, right at that moment, maybe for the first time ever: being bad – it can actually make you feel pretty good.

The Mermaid Diary

My legs felt hollow, my head fuzzily full, as we made our way round the lake – like that feeling you get when you step off the zippiest, screamiest, white-knuckliest rollercoaster ever.

Alice let out a brash laugh. "Ha, did you get a look at The Dragon's face?"

"She was furious," I agreed, but then I pictured her inhaling her lavender-blue Stella roses. "D'you feel a bit sorry for your gran?"

"As if!" Alice's jaw dropped. "You wouldn't feel bad for any of my family if you knew how they treated me!"

"Oh. Sorry." I fidgeted under her glare – she seemed to be checking if I meant it – until she switched to one of her sudden wide smiles, a regal hand-flourish around me. "Your turn next, Cinderella – " going all Fairy Godmother – "for your wish to come true."

I let out a weak laugh. "Huh, I'm not sure how you can make my mum notice me." I fiddled with my anorak cuffs, pressed my hair down as best as I could behind my ears.

"But I *told* you." Alice's brow furrowed in disappointment. "You just *reinvent* yourself; *change*. Create a story where you're the hero." She grabbed my arm to halt me; we'd arrived near the Mermaid Girls' sculpture again. Mist was circling it from the water, wide spectral fingers of grey now.

"Lay a trail of curiosity and intrigue to ensnare your mum like Hansel and Gretel." Her hands sprinkled imaginary breadcrumbs through the mottled air. "The witch only got them inside by building her house out of sweets and chocolates."

"Right." I was making the face I use in maths to look like I get the lesson. When I don't.

"Getting noticed is about *looks*." Alice flicked lightly at my old blue anorak.

"*Success*." She patted her jacket pocket where she'd earlier stashed that wad of cash.

"And *intrigue*." More breadcrumb-sprinkling. "*Then* your mum will sit up and take notice of you." A beckoning hand. "Give me your phone; we'll intrigue her now."

I cautiously passed my old Nokia to her.

"What the— Did you time-travel to get this dinosaur?"

I made an awkward laugh – followed soon after by some awkward poses. *Look like this; like that; no, do this*, Alice kept ordering, snapping loads of together-selfies, then applying what meagre filters I had to make my hair straighter and my shoulders narrower, nose daintier.

Until – *magic* – we almost looked identical. I mean it, really. I actually *looked* like Alice.

Hi, I'm Viv's new friend, Alice was already texting. Do you think we look like mermaids? We're trying to solve a Lake Mermaid mystery. Who knows – if we find her we might soon be rich and famous!

I watched her attach the best of the photos then scroll through my contacts till she found "Mum". And *hey presto* she sent it. Just like that. When I'd been dithering for an age about sending a message to Mum since she cancelled.

"Looks. Success. Intrigue. The message has it all," Alice said precisely, in her grown-up, newsreader voice.

Looks, success, intrigue: I tried scratching the three words into my head. I was learning more from her than I ever did in maths.

Alice shoved my phone in her jacket pocket. "Or else you'll be checking it constantly for a reply."

And she knew me so well already!

"Now we celebrate. With all the cake we can eat." Alice was back spinning through the fog spectres.

I was already late for helping Mimi at the shop, but – "All right!" Because, well, *cake*. And I knew what she meant: stealing that diary, running from The Dragon, messaging Mum – it did feel like we'd triumphed over something massive together.

I suggested we go to the old-lady haunt, Dorsal Dainties, instead of bustling Splash Tearooms, in case Erik saw me there (guilt made a quick sweep of my stomach). But Alice insisted. "You said they did the best hot chocolates!" And within minutes she was grandly conducting both hands across the colourful café display. "Choose anything you like! My treat!"

I could feel my eyes grow greedily wide. "Anything?" No one ever said that to me. Even Mimi had her limits when we came here for my birthday.

"Feed your heart's desire!" Alice plucked out that wad of banknotes from her jacket pocket, with a grin like the water sprites we sell in the shop.

I hesitated.

"What? Overdue pocket money," Alice said with a huffing noise. And she licked a finger and separated two purple notes, two brown. "Your winnings."

OK, I'll admit it, a bit of me was already thinking: I could pay off a bit of Mimi's bills; a new jacket to impress Mum; a phone that wasn't a hand-me-down-down-down – but ... "I can't take it."

"Why not?"

I thought for a moment I'd made her really angry – until she laughed. "Viv, my family have money coming out of their monstrous ears!" And she slammed two twenties down on the counter and began ordering. *Everything*.

I mean, everything. The deluxe hot chocolate that Mimi always complains is too expensive ("I'll make it for you at home", then never does), gingerbread mermaids, conch cream horns, marshmallow oyster shells, slices of rainbow Splendour sponge, Mermaid Crown doughnuts, tailfin cookies. I kid you not, I was salivating. It was like one of those feasts Eleni and I only dream about.

We took our trays through the insect hum of café voices to a table in a tucked-away corner, choosing to sit close to each other, our backs to everyone else.

Alice was gazing round like there was a bad smell in the air. I suppose the dust-trap shelves of shells and fishing nets, the painted wooden fish decorations, were a bit OTT. But we soon got giggling as the sugar rush kicked in. We competed eating doughnuts without licking our lips (I let Alice win) and we tried each other's conch horns and we both grew cream moustaches from the hot chocolate. I was starting to hope, *maybe Alice will forget about reading her dead aunt's diary and we can just keep having fun*. I was about to suggest, *Fancy a swim?* (because I could show her I was good at *something*), when Alice cut into my thoughts abruptly:

"Enough. We mustn't eat any more."

My mouth froze mid-bite of a delectable oozing marshmallow oyster shell.

"You never see fat mermaids." Alice removed the cream from her upper lip with one fierce tissue movement. She seemed cross at herself.

I tried to lick my own lips clean and suck in my stomach, reluctantly lowering the oozing oyster shell.

"I think it's time to read it now, don't you?" She took

a nervous breath, spreading out her fingers like she was about to play a piano concerto. I noticed they still looked sore, scraped and raw.

She withdrew them when she caught me staring. "I fell from the tyre swing," she said. "If you fly high, sometimes you have to take hits."

I nodded like I understood and reached to retrieve the diary from my swim bag.

"I told you, I'd not got past the front when The Dragon caught me." Alice flipped the diary over. "But look, I did see *this* – it's what brought me to your shop, Viv."

There was a price sticker on the back, branded with Enchanted Tails – £9.99 if you must know, which, *agreed*, seemed a bit steep for twenty years ago. Plus: "I didn't know we'd ever sold diaries. We leave that to Dive into Books."

"It's destiny!" Alice nudged me.

Something still felt a bit odd, but, "Destiny," I repeated. I suppose I did like the sound of it.

I watched Alice open the cover, carefully, as if it were some museum artefact.

1st August 2001
I thought I'd try writing a diary. Because I need to talk to someone. I don't know anyone in Lake Splendour any more.

Not since Mum and Dad forced me to go to Katie's boarding school. I hate it there, and I hate it here at home. Mum and Dad don't want me around (why did they even have children?) and Katie's become Worst Sister overnight.

I looked up briefly at Alice. The Mum, that was The Dragon, and "Worst Sister" Katie must be Alice's mum. Though Alice didn't look perturbed; her eyes focused seriously, unblinkingly on the page.

Katie totally ignores me at school now. This summer she won't even play with me. She says 15-year-olds can't hang out with 12-year-olds. Mum keeps telling Katie to take me out with her, so I'm "not making a nuisance" of myself at home. Katie pretends to, then she runs off, leaving me alone.

I don't understand it. We used to be close and tell each other everything. Now she'd rather be with some village children than me.

A spiky iceberg journeyed through my stomach as I pictured Eleni and Hero: I knew just how Stella felt.

4th August 2001
We used to go looking for the Lake Mermaid together in the holidays – now Katie says searching for mermaids is silly and

childish. Well, I've a good mind to tell on Katie and her new village friends – they're sneaking round smoking cigarettes and lighting campfires in the quarry woods! Yesterday they all made fun of my new lavender-blue mermaid cloak. They just laughed when I told them, "It's what mermaids wear on land!"

Alice's eyes had expanded into round discs. "I swear I saw someone wearing a blue cloak yesterday morning, up near the house." Now her mouth formed a circle. Mine trembled a little. I didn't know what to say – it was all getting too weird. We continued reading.

Katie didn't even stick up for me! How do I make people like me? I wish-wish-wish I could call the Lake Mermaid like those Splendour Mermaid Girls. Because I hate it here. I'm all alone.

I could almost hear Stella's tears between her words. I really didn't like this. I sucked in a breath as her dead diary voice continued, mainly talking about more things she hated: her spots, a boy who kept teasing her at school, ballet class. All she seemed to like were mermaids. Then…

8th August 2001
I've discovered something magical at the waterfall! A way to

the Mermaid World, I'm sure! Imagine it: Stella DeLacey, the
new Mermaid Girl! I told Katie – but she just sneered and said,
"Prove it!"

Fine! I will. Maybe if I find the Mermaid World, Katie will like
me again. We'll be close, like we used to be.

I'm going now, to bring back proof!

I let out my breath at the end of the page. "It's a bit
personal."

"Yes, because it's a diary!" Alice scoffed.

I fiddled with my mug. "I'm just not sure we should
be reading someone's private thoughts."

Gasp. "But, Viv, we have to keep reading to find out
what happened to my aunt! What she found out: *magical*,
she says!"

"Alice," I tried to choose my words carefully, so I
didn't make her cry again, "everyone says your Aunt
Stella *died* from searching for the Lake Mermaid."

"Yeah, and what if she didn't die?" There was a
sudden fierceness to her question. "There's no grave,
Viv! My mum and The Dragon *refuse* to talk about what
happened to Stella. But I've overheard The Dragon tell
Sleeping Grandpa that *Stella swims with mermaids now*.
She actually said that!" Glare, lingering. Furiously, she
turned the page – except there was only a stubby edge

next. Pages had been ripped out.

"What?! I bet The Dragon did that!" Alice exclaimed. "She thinks Stella's story belongs to her alone!"

The page after was blank.

I could feel my body relax with relief. I felt sorry for Alice – but now we could leave poor Stella DeLacey in peace.

"We'll never find out what happened to her." Alice sank in her seat. "My whole family keep secrets from me! They treat me like a little kid!"

"Sorry," I said, feeling suddenly a little lucky that Mimi talked to me like I was grown up. Well, OK, maybe not so much lately: distracted, keeping her money worries secret from me.

"Shall I show you the Mermaid Messenger game at Atlantis Arcades?" I attempted to cheer her up. "You get a personal message every time! No one else ever plays it, just me!"

Alice glared at me like I was talking gobbledygook. "I *saw* a blue cloak yesterday. Stella's saying she found a way to the Mermaid World. The Dragon's ripped pages out to hide the truth!" Another angry huff of breath and a punch of a huffy arm and Alice shoved the diary away from us. Knocking over what was left of my hot chocolate.

"Nooo! The Dragon will kill me!" A brown stain was spreading across the diary's cover.

I was already grabbing napkins, blotting the liquid. "It's all right, it's only a bit," I reassured her, fanning the pages before they stuck. Which was when I spotted it. Something was poking out from the later pages, like a bookmark. I opened the diary there – and Alice's hand found my arm, gripping it.

Stella's writing had resumed, but in a different colour ink: the same red as "The Mermaid Diary" on the front cover. The "bookmark" was a rectangular piece of parchment-style paper, singed at the edges. Drawn on it in pencil was a girl in a cloak with long thick hair. I slowly turned it over. The same girl was on the other side, but the cloak had gone; her hair was covering her naked chest … a scaly fishtail where her legs had been.

Pencil arrows were drawn at the bottom on both sides, as if it wanted you to keep turning.

Alice grabbed it from me. "What does it mean?"

Our eyes fled back to the red inked writing; more ragged, hurried.

10th August 2001

Welcome to The Mermaid Quest of Stella DeLacey.

Viv the
Great Pretender

Alice let out a little scream, bouncing up and down in her seat as our eyes shot down again.

YES! There IS a Lake Mermaid and I can prove it!

Me, friendless Stella DeLacey, I actually called the Lake Mermaid!

And soon I will join her in the Mermaid World!

Those tears, the hurt in Stella's voice – they'd been replaced by a breathless, excitable urgency…

Wait till Worst Sister Katie and those vile village children hear I'm not silly, that I was right to believe in mermaids! I've been chosen, not them! Ha, me! Serves them right for not letting me hang out with them.

…and err, nastiness.

There is a world beneath the lake and I'm going there! I AM the next Mermaid Girl!

ONLY read on if you're mermaid-worthy too… Well, are you?

The end of the page.

Neither of us spoke for the first few minutes.

Slowly, super-slowly, Alice said, "O-M-G!" Her grip on my arm tightened, vice-like. "Viv, this is bigger than I ever hoped! *Mermaid Quest*: my aunt actually *called* the Lake Mermaid from the water." Her eyes sparkled. "I was right all along!" Faster, furious seat-bouncing. "Doesn't it send tingles through you?"

I paused, checking my body for tingles: only the fizz from too much sugar that was now taking bites out of my gut. Because this was too spooky. I mean, it couldn't be true. Her aunt must have made it up. *Mermaids don't really exist. There's no Bigfoot, no Loch Ness Monster; snowmen can't turn abominable.* We only peddled the Mermaid Girls story about the Lake Mermaid for our tills. *Kerching.* I mean, OK, so no one knew the truth about where Lydia and Violet really disappeared to – but I'm pretty sure they didn't go visiting fish people who live under the lake.

Try telling that to Alice.

"I can't believe it. My aunt – finding the Mermaid World like those ugly girls in nineteen fourteen!"

"The Mermaid Girls weren't ugly." I shifted my Hobbit-feet awkwardly under the table.

Not that Alice was listening. Mouth agape, her eyes had moved from dreamy to bulging. "It means my Aunt Stella is still alive ... *swimming with mermaids*!"

No! I fidgeted with the parchment bookmark, flicking it back and forth quickly – until the legs on one side, tail on the other started to blur together like a magic trick.

Alice's bulging eyes popped – "It's Stella, becoming a mermaid!" – the seat bouncing was turning frenzied. "Viv, you're a total genius!"

My cheeks glowed. Despite our difference of mermaid opinion.

"Let's turn the page and find out more!"

She turned; I prayed: *Please, Stella, reveal – nah – no mermaid. The End. Goodnight.*

How wrong could I be?

Have you ever thought that you don't belong in this world? That you are different, magical?

That you are made for something better, a world where you live among queens, revered in an everlasting, magical life?

"Yes!" Alice burst out emphatically, then threw me an intense look, like she could actually hear the *Nope, never, not at all* in my head.

"I've always thought I was magical." Her lips pressed together with certainty.

I nodded. *Why wouldn't she?* Hair, skin, clothes, voice. *Magical.* Another fidget of my anorak cuffs.

Do you want to find out how I called the Lake Mermaid?

Alice: "Yes!"
Err, not really.

Will you follow everything I say and do?

"Yes!"

I'd rather not, if it's all the same with you.

You!

I pulled back. *Me?*

Who are YOU? Worst Sister Katie, is that you? Or maybe it's you, Nagging Mean Mum, trying to drag me home. Or maybe you're an adventurer like me, who's happened upon my diary (I wouldn't trust my mum not to have given this to a jumble sale once I've left).

Whoever you are, you must promise to abide by my rules, or the magic will NOT work. All right?

Alice bounced. "Absolutely!"

Absolutely not!

Before I leave for my new world, I am going to tell you how to call the Lake Mermaid. I will show you how to prove yourself worthy of entering the Mermaid World beneath Lake Splendour and swapping dull land legs ... for a tantalising tail.

But I won't make it easy for you. Why should I? I had to prove myself worthy by passing the same three tests of endurance as the Mermaid Girls. So should you.

OK, she was getting cocky now. All this mermaid-calling looked like it had gone to her head. I decided I preferred spotty, tearful, despairing Stella DeLacey. I sneaked a glance at Alice again. Concentration lines were multiplying on her forehead, eyes intent on Stella's words like it was an exam paper she had to complete – fast.

How to Call the Lake Mermaid
You must take three tests to prove yourself worthy.
Test 1: COURAGE
Test 2: REBELLION
Test 3: TRANSFORMATION

If I wasn't getting creeped out enough already, Stella had made a little drawing beside each of the three words. A mermaid tail (courage), a conch shell (rebellion), a knife dripping with red ink (transformation). The last one turned my legs to jelly. "I go funny around the sight of blood," I confessed. Our school nurse made a note of all future dissections after I fainted that time in biology. I tried to lighten the mood. "It's like getting Brownie badges."

Alice flashed me *pay attention* teacher-eyes.

DO NOT read on – unless you solemnly PROMISE to complete each test.

Warning: once you seek out the Lake Mermaid, you cannot turn back.

You might want to consider your choice a moment. Do you want to venture forward on a quest to transform yourself and your life?

OR NOT?

I repeat: Once you call her, there is NO RETURN!

The capitals of the last two words made me jolt. *Now* I felt a tingling, but not the good kind – more like when Eleni and I watched that *Goosebumps* film. *No return.* A game of *Jumanji* was starting in my mind. "What does she mean? That you *can't* turn back?"

Alice flicked at her hair. "She probably means why would you! Who wouldn't want to swap this poxy world for a magical one?" She rolled her eyes at the wooden fish stuck to the wall beside us then reclasped my arm, so tightly this time it actually hurt. "We have to do this; we must." Her voice suddenly sounded as deadly serious as Stella's. "I want to change, don't you?"

A tail for my legs?

I didn't answer immediately. The noises of the café – the chit-chat, the grind of the coffee machine, the music

104

in the background – all seemed to get louder, like my ears wanted to remind my brain of normal life. What Stella just said in the diary: *Not Real*. I mean, escaping a dragon's lair and messaging Mum a cool photo and eating more cakes than Marie Antoinette – that was fun, thrilling. But this?

"What's that face for?" Alice was examining me. "Viv, if we get proof the Lake Mermaid exists, you'll become a worldwide celebrity and get noticed by everyone." Her hands shaped a headline in the air. "The New Mermaid Girls."

"And when I choose to disappear into another world, my parents will finally regret what they did to me—" Alice broke off, fingers furiously crumbling the last mermaid gingerbread I'd had my eyes on. "Not that I'll care. I'll be swimming underwater with Aunt Stella!"

She flicked a "forget-it" hand as I asked, "What *did* they do to you?" She was too busy with her hypnotic eyes, moving closer to me, till they merged to form a Cyclops.

"Viv, your mum won't be able to resist you. Isn't that what you want?" Her breath smelled of chocolate and ginger.

I thought again of Mimi worrying about the shop; the MPs' evil sabotage; Eleni's treachery. If I could get

Mum here, she'd make everything better. Except: *There is. No. Mermaid.* Sure, there were those 1960s scientists who picked up sonar sounds with the same resonance as singing; blurry Lake Mermaid photos were always doing the rounds on social media. But no evidence had ever been taken *seriously*. "We'd never get enough proof." I smiled weakly.

Alice drew a sharp breath. "I thought you said you believed in the Lake Mermaid?" Her deep-sea blues were watery again. "Viv, were you just pretending to please me?"

"Pretending? Course not," my voice warbled, shame turning my cheeks scarlet. "I'm no good at pretending." The sugar in my stomach sprouted sharp teeth. "I just need the loo," I quickly excused myself.

Forget rollercoaster, I was on the waltzer, going round and round, spinning faster and faster. I splashed my face with water from the cold tap in the toilets and gazed up at my flushed reflection above the sink. My hair had gone coil-crazy from the wet air outside: more witch-hunter than mermaid-caller. *Admit to Alice you don't believe in mermaids*, I tried speaking sternly to myself. *You're not good enough at pretending to pretend you're* not *pretending!* Calm breath. I tamed my hair and returned to the table.

I'd confess and suggest other – far less creepy – ways to enjoy summer: penny drops, ice creams, rowing boats. My determination wavered just as I reached her. "Hey, is that my phone?"

Alice was swiping at it under the table. Seeing me, she jumped – then that wide smile. "Look who texted you!"

My heart made a tennis-ball bounce in my chest. I rushed forward.

Hello, Viv's friend, Mum had written. That sounds cool. I always wanted to get rich and famous from finding the mermaid!

"You did?" I said to the phone.

I didn't know you had it in you, Viv. Impressed. Keep me updated!

I grinned up at Alice. It had worked, like Alice said it would. Breadcrumbs of intrigue; filtered looks; a sniff of success!

I started to seat-bounce myself. It was one of those Eureka moments you see scientists getting in films. Like I'd been doing it wrong all these years, being me, myself; *quiet*, *polite*, *should-speak-up-more-in-class* Vivien, campaigning against littering and lousy school dinners.

Impressed. I should have worked harder at pretending long ago!

My stomach was back *whizz-pop-banging*. I released a

decisive breath and put my palm flat on the diary. This was no *Jumanji* quest or *Goosebumps* horror, just made-up stuff in a tragic girl's life. But … it might just solve my problems.

"Alice, if we were to take these three tests, do you think you could post about it?" I thought back to that video of *All-hail-Hero*'s that Eleni forwarded. I could fight back against their anti-mermaid campaign. "Why don't we start a new social media account to promote the Lake Mermaid?" People would listen to Alice.

"Viv, that's a great idea!"

My cheeks were back warm and glowing.

"Then let's do it!" I said. Just maybe, by following a quest to find our Lake Mermaid, we could put Lake Splendour back on the map. More tourists for Enchanted Tails. More excitement for Mum! And how hard could it be? After all, to show Bigfoot exists all you do is make a massive footprint.

Alice reached for my hand. She didn't seem to mind that it was still damp. "Isn't this thrilling? A whole new world awaits us, Viv!"

So what if it wasn't true, if the Lake Mermaid wasn't real. This was what I'd done even before I could read and write – lived and breathed our fishy, fantastical lake legend.

"But we probably shouldn't mention the diary," I said quickly, picturing another Dragon chase.

"Agreed. Our secret." Alice gestured zipping up her mouth then pushed out a pinkie and I gripped it with mine. "A pact," she said. "A promise between us to see this through to the end."

"Deal," I agreed, wishing she'd let my pinkie go now; it was starting to hurt a little.

It was only later, when I was hanging my swim stuff out to dry ("Otherwise you forget and it goes crusty," nagged Mimi), that my fingers met with something papery. I opened my swim bag wider to look inside: two twenties and two ten-pound notes, folded into a tight, neat square. *My winnings.* Alice must have stashed them there when I was in the toilet in Splash Tearooms. I glanced up at my shelf of "they're-plotting-something" mermaid dolls from Mum's travels, as if they might snitch on me. The Hawaiian mo'o doll was looking especially traitorous.

Pause to think – before I hurriedly hid the money in my sock drawer.

I couldn't believe how much had happened to me in just a few days. Meeting Alice, I was already "transforming": more successful, intriguing, richer... The kind of daughter Mum wanted.

Something Stirs Beneath the Water

I awoke to the sound of buzzing insects, my hands flapping at the air round my face – until I realised – *oh* – the buzzing insects were in fact my phone.

I'd never heard it so busy. I sat up in bed to reach for it and – *whoa* – Alice had already done what I suggested.

@NewMermaidGirls

#MermaidsAreReal

#LakeMermaidQuest

No way! Two hundred and twelve followers. In one night! (Eleni and I didn't even make twelve with *Oi, Stop Your Littering!*). I could literally sense my chest expanding with possibility and pride. Alice had posted the best pictures of us and I sort of looked OK (even if I didn't look like me). She'd tagged our cake feast with #BestFriends and #BestHotChocolate and my stomach briefly pinched at the thought of Eleni or Erik seeing it, before – excited squeeze – Alice saw me as Best Friend already?

The insects kept on buzzing while I got dressed. *Waltzers and rollercoasters*: so this was how the Princess Table felt, I smiled to myself, sneaking into the kitchen without disturbing Mimi.

Fail.

"You're up early!" Mimi said with a jump. She was hurriedly replacing old-looking items into a long metal box on the kitchen table, as if I'd caught her with illegal contraband. Then, "Is that lip gloss? You're too young for make-up, love."

I pretended not to hear. I'd taken extra care with my appearance. No anorak today. Alice would be wanting more photos to post; more followers, more "likes". Not that I was going to tell Mimi I was hanging out with the girl she thought was too *extra-ordinary* for me.

"And that skirt's for special, Vivien, not every day. We don't have money for new clothes right now."

Right never.

"What's that?" I said to distract her, nodding my head at her box of contraband. It looked attic-old.

Mimi pulled a "nothing" face. "Just some items of Lydia and Violet's from the tourist office archives. Exciting!" she added, though her eyes seemed to disagree: *Disastrous!*

I peered across her into the metal box. "Wow, is that Violet's suffragette sash?" I could see a piece of striped material, purple, green and white. "The one with 'Votes for Women' that she wears in the exhibition photograph?"

Mimi drew the box away from me. "Sorry, love – afraid it's for festival committee eyes only. Until we decide how we might use it all." *Exciting!* her smile said. *Disastrous!* her eyes disagreed.

"Why can't they display her sash all the time? So what if the tourists aren't interested?" I said. Alice's boldness was rubbing off on me.

"Well, the committee do talk about trialling a different type of display," she said uncertainly, as if any trial would be life and death, not local history. Her eyes made an optical sigh. "It's all a bit complicated, Vivien, love."

112

So much for always talking to me like a grown-up. I began reaching for the cornflakes when I spotted she'd missed something on the table. I darted to grab it first. An old postcard – the picture on the front a grotesque monster. Half-woman, half-demon, with wild snake-like hair, fanged teeth and shrivelled eyes. "*Your leader*" was scrawled in black ink in one corner. "What is it?" I was flipping it over as Mimi's hand shot out. I only had time to glance briefly at some more old-fashioned writing before she'd whipped it away from me. But long enough to read:

"*IF YOU ANSWER HER CALL TO FIGHT, YOU WILL CHANGE INTO A MONSTER LIKE HER! SHE WILL DRAG YOU DOWN AND DESTROY YOU!*"

"I said, *not* for your eyes." Mimi frowned as she replaced the postcard in the box and slammed the lid shut.

I was remembering what Erik had said, about overhearing committee discussions about the Mermaid Girls being imprisoned. "*Answer her call...* Whose? The Lake Mermaid's?" I demanded, a small shake to my voice.

It was Mimi's turn to pretend she hadn't heard me. "I must hurry, get this box back to the tourist office and then open the shop, and you –" her sighing eyes turned mithering – "remove that lip gloss." A brusque tone to her voice she rarely used; *conversation over.*

Maybe Alice was right: the Oldies kept secrets … the Oldies wanted to control us.

Hallelujah. Sunshine had returned outside as I made my way to meet Alice on the lakeshore, yellow substituting grey and making everything look more cheerful. The fog had receded into scraps of fine lace above the mountains; the water reflecting the sun in sparkling blue and silver jewels. It worked its miracle – tourists were swarming on the shore like ants round a dropped ice lolly. Day-trippers in swimsuits pretending the pebble shore was a proper beach; splashing, paddling, shrieking. The ice-cream kiosk on the promenade was open and tourists were lining up on the jetty to rent a rowing boat to "*Spot the Lake Mermaid on the water!*" The bandstand was hosting a choir singing "Walking on Sunshine". *Yep*, the weather even made *that* seem possible.

"Ready for our mermaid adventure?" Alice arrived (late again), wearing denim shorts (fashionably frayed) and a bright-blue sweatshirt with a designer logo (the kind Mimi complains is "Paying for the privilege of advertising their brand!"). It made me glad I'd reapplied the lip gloss once I'd left the shop. Though my "best" skirt suddenly seemed as outdated as our promenade flower baskets.

"You did an amazing job on those posts," I complimented her straightaway.

Alice gave me a look like she already knew it. "I tagged loads of influential people I know," she said with a hand-waft. "Looks, success, intrigue: see, works a treat.

"Let's send an extra photo to your mum," she added, ushering me into another selfie, sunlit this time. Her filters were much better than mine (latest iPhone, *course*): sparkly mermaid hair and massive Disney-doll eyes. I almost looked mermaid-beautiful.

Next, Alice pulled out Stella's diary from her (expensive-looking) leather rucksack, announcing to the cover, "We're ready," as if the pages were Stella herself. I had wondered if she might have sneaked a look overnight (I mean, it's what I'd do) – but the parchment-bookmark was still where we left it and that look was back on Alice's face, like she was taking it all *deadly* seriously.

TEST ONE: COURAGE
Are you courageous enough to fight and change?
  Here's your clue for what you must do...

115

I chewed my lips, accidentally removing all the gloss. *Fight and change*. It was reminding me of that postcard Mimi just snatched off me … *MONSTER … SHE WILL DRAG YOU DOWN AND DESTROY YOU.*

Go to where the water runs fast and furious, where currents change and the flow fights back.
Look down at what you can't see.
Keep seeking and you shall find.

"Water? Does she mean we should go on the lake, Viv?"

I liked the way Alice looked to me for answers. I didn't want to let her down. I forgot the postcard and stared out at the lake: a blue-green today. "*Fast and furious*: she might mean the lake waterfall? Didn't she mention it in her diary?" We flicked back to the earlier pages in blue ink to find: *I have discovered something magical at the waterfall.*

"She did! You're *so* clever, Viv!"

It wasn't that hard really, but, still, I let myself bask in another face-glow as I added, "Legend says Lake Splendour fisherfolk would sometimes see the mermaid in the waterfall." I frowned, recalling the ticking-off The Dragon gave me in their garden. "The Dra—Your gran – she said she owns the waterfall?"

"Stupid woman. Only because it starts from the edge of their wood," Alice scoffed. "You can't *own* a waterfall. Come on, Viv, what are we waiting for?" She grabbed my hand – hers was rough and raw, like she'd fallen off her tyre swing again – and began pulling me across the pebbles. She didn't stop, not even when I stumbled, and – don't ask me how – somehow she managed to get us straight to the top of the jetty queue (new tip: pretend you know someone at the front).

Once we were water-bound (in a rowing boat named *Lorelei*), it took us a while to leave the shallows. We were both rowing, but our elbows kept hitting each other and our oars were out of sync, turning in eternal circles. In the end I told Alice, "I'll row alone if you like." Too eagerly, she switched to sit opposite me, slumping back and trailing her fingers through the water; model-in-a-fashion-shoot. I did wish she'd put her life jacket on though. She was right, they did look awful, but, as Mimi would say, "Better buoyant than in a body bag."

"To the wondrous waterfall and away from the poxy village of plebs!" Alice was playing captain. "Faster, Viv!"

And I wanted her to think I was good at it, so I kept rowing and rowing, charging through lily pads with fronds like jellyfish tentacles, speeding alongside a sudden streak of gold and blue kingfisher. The sun seemed to get hotter and sweat was soon prickling across my scalp. My face was a furnace and my arms were aching by the time we passed beneath Alice's grandparents' house. It looked even more spectacular from down here, looming tall from its land of giants.

"Who's that watching?" I said, spotting a lanky outline of a figure at the edge of their lawn, blurred into a bluish hue by bright sunlight.

"Probably someone who works for The Dragon. *Monsters Incorporated.*" Alice cast a dramatic hand-waft.

"*I'm watching you, Wazowski. Always watching,*" I mimicked, and – result! – I finally got Alice laughing.

"Oi, sailor, who said you could stop rowing?" Alice splashed me and I kicked my oar out to splash her back. Two ospreys appeared from nowhere, swooping freely above our heads. We'd left all the other boats behind; it was just me and Alice. And despite my achy-sweaty-furnace discomfort, it became one of those moments you wish you could freeze-frame forever. *Welcome to your new life, Vivien.*

I followed orders and resumed fast rowing. Soon after, we reached the waterfall: a narrow veil of silvery-blue falls thrashing down from an overhang of quarry cliff – that I now knew was The Dragon's land – to meet the lake. Shielding my eyes, I gazed up to its full height, watching the light flit like will-o'-the-wisps through the water, when there was movement at the top. A flash of blue. That lanky figure again? "Didn't you say you saw a blue-cloaked figure the other day?" I said hesitantly – regretting it instantly as Alice bounced around, swaying the boat. "Show me! Where!"

"Nothing," I replied quickly. It had already gone. "Probably just the sunshine playing tricks."

"Closer! Get us closer!" Alice demanded.

"We can't. It's too dangerous." I pointed at where the waterfall hit the lake. "See the whirlpool? It can tug you into the eroded rock beneath and trap you there." I'd learned that in geography (when Eleni and I weren't getting sent out over Brokenwind). I pulled the oars in and let the boat bob and float instead. Alice shrugged and rested her cheek dreamily on her arm, one hand tracing a path through the water. At first I thought she was humming along with the musical sound of the cascade, until I caught words whispered under her breath.

"We call to you, Lake Mermaid.

"We want to be one with you.

"Show yourself to us.

"Summon us."

There was a rhythm to her voice – like some strange incantation or a holy prayer.

"Take us to your world."

It was sending cold threads darting beneath my clammy skin – when I noticed her hand near her cheek, fingers like pistons, moulding something. A glimpse of a familiar china face between her thumb and forefinger. A naiad wishing doll – like we sold in our shop.

"We want to be powerful like you, Lake Mermaid," the prayer finished.

I drew back a little. "Did you get that doll from Enchanted Tails?" The image was clear in my head, of Alice touching a naiad doll the day I first met her. She never bought one.

Alice glanced down at her hand and frowned as if she hadn't meant for me to see the doll there. "We must find the Lake Mermaid, Viv," she said distractedly, almost feverishly. "We must make sure she hears our call."

I said nothing. I stared out at the water, trying to find a polite way to ask *Did you steal that doll from my shop?* without accusing her, when—

"I've not been completely honest with you." The doll had disappeared and Alice was gazing directly at me.

"What do you mean?" I licked my gloss-lost lips; they felt bone-dry.

"The reason I'm in Lake Splendour ... is because I got expelled from school."

My whole mouth felt parched; I wished we'd brought water to drink. "What did you get expelled for?" My voice a squeak.

Alice looked up at me from under her eyelids; a half-smile. "You sure you want to know?"

"Yes." *No.* It was just a coincidence, surely, that the sun briefly travelled behind a cloud, casting a looming, shadowy shape over the lake.

"For bad behaviour." Alice made a half-laugh sound. "Whatever, it's a story for another time," she said teasingly. "The point is, Mum says, 'I'm not paying for any more expensive boarding schools for you, madam.'" She imitated her mother as a deranged witch – then smacked the surface of the water hard with her trailing hand, spraying water. "She lives in Singapore. Dad lives in France, with his new *belle petite famille*." Her parcel-bow mouth twisted oddly. "My *denouement*? I've been dumped on The Dragon forever, to go to school here."

"You're not just here for summer?"

"But I am!" Her whole face reignited. "Because – I'm not going to stay *here*, I'm going to find Aunt Stella and the Mermaid World." She withdrew her hand from the lake, dripping water as she leaned towards me. "I'm so lucky to have met you, Viv. We have each other. That's all that matters." Those hypnotic eyes were busy again, peering into mine. "I want us to be close friends, the closest. Sharing every secret."

The sweat prickling my scalp was intensifying, spreading hot and itchy all over my body.

Alice's brow furrowed. "I can trust you, can't I?"

The itchiness turned to embarrassment. I took a confessional breath. My turn to come clean. "I've not been one hundred per cent truthful," I said, more sheepish than, well, a sheep. "But I do want to be close too," I added hurriedly, fidgeting with the oar handles. "I've sort of been … I dunno … pretending a bit, to believe in the mermaid."

Alice glanced at me askance. She leaned back, pushing her elbows against the stern of the boat, nodding slowly, like she was absorbing the information. A sudden shrill call from above: those ospreys were circling, black crosses against the pale-blue sky.

"I forgive you," Alice said abruptly. She had the look of a priest too. "Seeing is believing, for many people," she added, even more priest-like. "You'll believe fully once we call her."

I nodded cautiously. I wanted to ask her again about the naiad wishing doll, about why she got expelled, but we were drifting too close to the waterfall. Hurriedly, I focused on rowing us away, while, "Let's swim!" Alice exclaimed brightly. "If we want to seek a mermaid like the diary says, we should get wet." Like she'd already forgotten about my confession.

"Swimming's not recommended this far from shore," I told her, heaving on the oars to reverse the boat. "Too many weeds. Plus, it's really deep here."

"Viv! Don't you ever get tired of following the rules?" She stood up, rocking the boat, and stripped down to just a T-shirt and pants. Sandals off, throwing tanned legs over the side.

"Don't, Alice!" I said as she gasped back fiercely, "Viv! Did you just see that – *there* – moving through the water!"

I followed where she was pointing – an area dense with weeds, long and shiny like mermaid hair and swaying in harmony. "It was a fish, probably. We've pike the size of small dogs." I was more concerned with keeping the boat balanced. "Or an eel. We get them this far out."

"Eels?" Alice gazed back into the water with a visible tremor. "Maybe you're right. Let's swim closer to shore." She began to pull one leg in, looping the other round as something seemed to grab at her foot, yanking at her, sending the boat lurching.

Another violent jolt from beneath, a brief cry of pain, and within seconds Alice was dragged off the side like a released anchor, plummeting down into the water.

"Alice?" I screamed, lunging across, boat pitching, desperately trying to see beneath the crowded grey-green weeds. She was nowhere. Alice – she'd gone! In a panic I ripped off my life jacket and tugged off my trainers. I'd done my life-saving course at swim club: I knew it was only minutes before blood stops pumping oxygen to your brain. I didn't think of eels and whirlpools and weeds, I just dived, straight down into knife-sharp cold water.

Where was she? I couldn't see anything below either. A greenish black; zipping shadows of fish; dancing weeds, crowding me like an angry mob.

I burst upwards for breath. That old postcard Mimi had was back in my head, half-woman, half-demon: *SHE IS A MONSTER! SHE WILL DRAG YOU DOWN AND DESTROY YOU.*

"Alice!" She'd still not surfaced. Down again; another frantic search. The dense weeds were starting to take on different shapes – mermaid shapes – when something gripped on to my ankle, clenching, ensnaring; it was dragging me down. I opened my mouth to cry and it immediately filled with gritty, bitter lake water.

A violent *kick-kick-kick* to free my trapped foot, thrusting my arms up in a reverse knife dive – breaking the water gasping for air. Coughing, spluttering; eyes blurry.

"Viv!"

Alice was up at last, clutching on to the other side of the boat, deep-breath-gasping too, her face pale, eyes big, hair plastered to her head. She shrieked – another splash, arms flailing as if she was fighting with something underneath.

I pushed my head down into a fast crawl to reach her – just as her head broke the surface again.

"Viv, follow her!" she shouted, spitting water, her voice caught somewhere between terror and thrill. She struck a course towards the waterfall.

I tried to see what she was seeing – "Alice, *stay away!*" – imagining a giant eel or a murderous shoal of pike in the murky shadows directly beneath us as, swimming fast, I followed her into the thrashing water. Our bodies soon became whirlpool fodder, pummelled and punched as if we were in a washing machine. Alice's head was disappearing again.

I lunged, gripping on to her, a fierce side-stroke out of the falls' watery clutches.

"Was it her?" was the first thing Alice said as we faced

each other, sodden and shaking and back inside the boat, legs bound by algae-gloopy reeds and ribbon-like weeds.

"Pike or eels," I said, my voice chattering in tune with my teeth.

"*No* – something *grabbed* at me, Viv. Took me down."

"The weeds," I said. "I told you, they're hazardous, like living rope."

I could see from Alice's face that she didn't believe me. I wasn't sure any more myself. Could weeds clench, ensnare, drag us both down? My eyes fled back to the top of the waterfall, thinking of that strange, lanky, bluish figure as a shrill noise sent me glancing in the opposite direction. The two black crosses were still directly above us. Their circling suddenly seemed more sinister than before. It was like we were prey.

"She clutched on to me so tightly. Then she let go," Alice was saying, her voice as frayed as the denim shorts she was tugging back on, making the boat sway again.

"It was the weeds," I repeated. *It didn't feel like weeds; stronger, fiercer.* "Alice, what if the Lake Mermaid isn't beautiful?" *You don't believe in mermaids.* "Not nice?"

"Not *nice*? Viv, she's powerful! She's a lake mermaid, a mystical creature – not Mary Poppins! And not beautiful?" she added with a blunt laugh. "Is the pope a Catholic?" She began wringing out the hem of her vest top. "Though that whirlpool was ready to swallow me whole like a giant mouth." She stopped and looked intently at me. I couldn't tell if it was lake water or tears in her eyes. "You saved my life, Viv. You're incredible."

"Oh, not really," I said, the warm glow on my cheeks *not* sunshine. I zipped on my life jacket – my body still shaky – and started to row us back to shore.

Silence. Just the swish of the oars; the wash of the water; the sway of evergreens on the hillsides. Lake water was congealing around my eyes, a clay-like film in my mouth. My *best* skirt was now sodden and sticking to my legs (*sorry, Mimi*). I couldn't get the smell of lake water out of my nostrils, the sensation of seeing Alice twice yanked down, as if by an alligator or a shark – then I heard something, faint and feathery, on the air.

Cautiously, I looked over both shoulders, left, right, half expecting to see a broad, sparkly tail breaking the surface.

"*Viv-ee-en...*"

I tightened my grip on the oars, breath catching in my chest, furiously scanning the water closest to us.

"What is it?" Alice's lips still looked blue.

"I th-thought I heard my name," I said, instantly feeling stupid.

A shriek like a kettle whistle made me jump. The

black-cross birds were swooping even closer.

"Must've imagined it." *It was the wind; the oars on water; the waves.*

Alice's lips were slowly returning from blue to pink by the time we approached the jetty. Just spotting the tourists licking their 99 flakes and chomping on mermaid rock, hearing the piped music from Atlantis Arcades, the shrieks from paddling children – it was enough to plant me back on earth. I'd allowed Stella's diary to spook me, *Jumanji* nonsense to slide under my skin. *This* was normal: selling fake – *fake* – mermaids to the tourists.

I smiled back at Alice, pleased to have convinced myself that I'd imagined that creepy voice, the strong grip of the weeds.

Alice was already grinning widely, her eyes raised above mine. "Viv, oh, your *hair*!"

I patted the prickly hedge that was on my head. The warm lake breeze had dried it already.

"Yeah, it does that if it gets wet," I said apologetically, "and if I don't use heaps of conditioner. I have to wear a cap when I swim."

"What a nightmare."

I nodded, turning a different kind of pink in annoyance at my hair – *why did you have to choose my head to sit on? –* as I chucked our boat's rope to the attendant.

"Was that the test, do you think? *Courage* – to enter the waterfall whirlpool?" Alice said, wobbling as she rose. "Do you think we passed? Will the Lake Mermaid be pleased?"

I looked back out across the lake. Those ospreys had completely disappeared, like I'd imagined them too. Though in the distance the fine lace scraps of fog that had been hanging over the mountains seemed to have become spectral again. As if they were waiting for the right moment to move back on to shore.

Weeds, wind, eels, that's all, I reminded myself as we climbed back on to the jetty.

The Shell Grotto

I had to spend the next few days helping Mimi. The shop was filling with boxes to unpack ready for the festival, now only one week away. Wooden huts were arriving along the promenade, soon to be filled with chocolate mermaid tails and edible shell necklaces, plastic crowns and tridents and nylon wigs galore. There were posters tied to lampposts, advertising how to enter the Mermaid Crown and the Lake Race. But the MPs' propaganda was also spreading through the village. Locals kept coming into the shop to ask if the Crown was actually going ahead and we'd already seen a slump in mermaid-costume sales, making Mimi even more tetchy and distracted.

Thank goodness @NewMermaidGirls was growing its following. I'd even noticed a nice comment from Princess Table Sahana (I bet she wished she'd thought of it!). The quest was more vital than ever: posts to fuel mermaid fever and fight back against the poisonous MPs. Plus, that morning I'd got a reply from Mum to the last photo Alice had sent her: Disney-big eyes and long mermaid hair. You look amazing, almost like I'm looking in the mirror, Viv! I kept widening my eyes to huge, pulling painfully at the ends of my hair. Now I just had to summon the courage to plead for her to come for the Lake Race.

It was Thursday when Alice and I finally met to look at the next section of the diary.

"*Test two: REBELLION*," Alice was reading aloud from the page.

We were at the Mermaid Girls sculpture again (Alice late, again); there was more bird poo on Lydia's bronze head. The air surrounding us was a little less yellow, a need-a-jacket chill. Today's lake a stone-grey. The ice-cream kiosk hadn't opened yet and a group of Year Sixes were using the bandstand as a skatepark.

Do you have what it takes to be rebellious? Here's your clue for what you need to find:

Go to where the magic starts.

Stand back to back with the Lake Mermaid.

Discover the gift that will help you see who you can truly be.

Finishing reading the clue, Alice looked up. "What do you think, Viv?" Hypnotic eyes pinning mine.

I sucked in a long breath. Three days ago my suggestion had ended up with us getting dragged into a death-defying whirlpool and hallucinating voices.

"*Viv?*" Alice was waiting impatiently.

"Err, well, the sign to the Shell Grotto says '*This way to mermaid magic*'," I offered. "And there's the Lake Mermaid statue there, if it means back to back literally…"

It seemed another obvious one as I said it, yet Alice squealed and clapped like I'd answered the million-pound question. "Viv, you're unbelievable!"

Cue warm glow. Pleasing Alice was becoming as addictive as marshmallow oyster shells.

An arm looped through mine and she was dragging me into a run, round the lake and into the dark, jagged rock tunnel. Alice never seemed to walk anywhere. Passing the mermaid-shaped sign, she got out her phone, filming us entering the grotto. Newsreader voice, volume up. "We're just two girls on a quest to call the Lake Mermaid and find the Mermaid World. Join us as we journey through caves and battle deep water."

"Caves and deep water?" I mouthed at her.

Alice swatted a *shush*, *performing* hand.

Looks, success, intrigue, remember? I silently chastised myself. Alice did all three so well.

There were only a few visitors in the grotto as we entered. "What do you reckon, maybe 'rebellious' means stealing one of the shells?" Alice whispered. She struck out a red penknife from her pocket.

I recoiled sharply at the sight of it. A loud *no way* was erupting in my head, but I kept my answer pleasant. "We probably shouldn't…" I didn't want to make Alice cry again. "Toby Short in Year Eight got cautioned by the police when he tried to slice out a giant cowrie."

"Good for Toby Short!" Alice flicked out the blade and began trailing it over the bumps of shells sticking out from the wall, a sharp *tap-scrape* sound. "Remember, we're supposed to be proving we're rebellious, Viv!" She scowled. "You won't get excitement if you remain in your cage and follow what the Oldies say."

My warm glow had gone thoroughly ice-cold. I'd displeased her. She thought I was a wimp. I tried harder. *Back to back with the Lake Mermaid*, Stella had said. I faced the statue: perfect stone features. Even her long stone hair managed to appear luxurious – like Mum's, I was thinking, as the idea came to me. I whipped my gaze around the grotto. It really wasn't allowed, there were even signs that said *"Paddling prohibited!"* *Be rebellious*, I told myself under my breath, and I flicked my hair back like Alice (forgetting my hair's not the flicky kind) and moved to the low wall of the trickling fountain. I surreptitiously removed my trainers, socks off, trying not to think of diving into the lake; that feeling of being dragged down.

My feet made their first splash of water. Ow, it was freezing.

"Lass, you can't do that!" a day-tripper nearby called out.

I froze, flushed, seriously reconsidering *rebellious*. But then I heard an Alice-squeal of pleasure. It was enough to send me wading calf-deep out of view round the statue of the Lake Mermaid, soles slipping and pinching over a slimy carpet of copper and silver wishes. Yes, the tutting and critical commentary continued from behind, but oh – this felt exhilarating, to be doing what I shouldn't. *Me*, who did everything to avoid a telling-off at school! Maybe I was changing. *Mum, I'm becoming more like you!*

Splash. Alice was stepping into the fountain as well. And she didn't look like she cared one jot about the tutting. "Can you see anything?" she hissed.

Turning back to back with the Lake Mermaid, I ducked down to check the larger shells cemented to the wall opposite. Alice examined the floor. "There must be thousands of coins here."

"Shells too." My "rebel" was quickly waning. Whatever "gift" we were supposed to find, it was like looking for a needle in a haystack.

"Tutting voice" beyond the statue was loudly discussing our behaviour with another: "I've a good mind to go and tell someone." I was about to suggest to Alice, politely, that we give up, when my eye caught a glint of something: a contrasting green inside a bright-pink conch.

"Alice, here," I said, my chest fizzing with discovery. I pushed two fingers inside the shell's smooth mouth, jostling it out.

A jewel: hexagonal, transparent green. "It's like the one in Stella's drawer," I said with whispered awe.

"What are you talking about?"

I glanced at Alice. She was frowning.

"Stella had one just like this, didn't she?" I frowned too. "It was in her drawer beneath her diary. I thought you'd have seen it?"

A fierce shake of her head. "I never saw any green jewel in Stella's drawer." Her bright eyes seemed to assess me, grow sharp. "Viv, did you take it from Stella's room? Did you just put this here?" Sharp to wounded, blue eyes filling again. "Is this what you meant out on the lake, about how you've been pretending?"

My face grew hot, like I *was* guilty. "No, never. I left it in the drawer, I promise."

"I'd understand. We're rebels. We steal what we need." Alice's eyes were narrowing, like those lake ospreys'. As if she'd been witness to me in Stella's bedroom, when I'd been tempted to take the beautiful jewel from the drawer. She licked her lips ferociously. "You *have* to tell me the truth." She was examining me as if she was trying to see truths behind my eyes. "Do you promise on your life you're not tricking me, Viv?"

My neck stiffened. "I promise."

Alice drew back, her blue eyes softening again. She gazed at the stone with me. "It is beautiful."

I nodded. "Weird though," I said, enjoying the cool

feel of it in my hand, the way its glass surface caught both shadow and light. "I mean, who'd just leave this here?"

Stupid question.

"The Lake Mermaid, of course," Alice answered immediately. "She knows we're searching for her! A gift for passing two tests – Stella must have been given one too!" She nudged my arm. "Here, hold it up."

It had been my instinct when I'd seen Stella's jewel too. I raised it towards the light from the grotto window until our green reflections appeared, small, yet large – almost magical.

"*Discover the gift that will help you see who you can be.*" We repeated Stella's diary words right at the same time, giggled – then I gasped. A third shape had joined our reflection.

Stop the Mermaid Crown

I glanced around sharply until – sigh of relief – it was only the stone head of the Lake Mermaid, looming over us. My feet numb and cold, I started to lead us out of the water, preparing for more tutting. Instead, I heard a surprised:

"Vivien?"

My heart skittered at my name – almost dropping the jewel in the water – before I saw who it was.

"Eleni?"

"What on earth are you doing in the fountain?" She was staring with open-mouthed bafflement at me and Alice standing ankle-deep in water. Behind her, I could see the Mighty Protestors crowding into the grotto. *All-hail-Hero* in the lead flanked by her trendy friends: Khalil, lashes thick with mascara; Emma with the diamanté eye patch; Jadon and his nose stud; Skye with blue-tipped braids.

It was Thursday. I'd completely forgotten. That video Eleni had sent me; the *Stop the Mermaid Crown* action was starting today.

"You shouldn't be in there, Vivien!" Eleni placed one hand on her hip, like she was Sensible Grown-up and I was a toddler caught with my hands covered in cake. Rebellious Viv deflated like a month-old balloon. I noticed she had on a new purple puffer jacket (similar to Hero's), that same pin-badge on her chest: *STOP the Mermaid Crown!* (like Hero); a tiny plait in her fringe (*Hero*). It was like they were in some tribe together. My stomach made its own small plait, parcel tight.

"Have you been getting my messages?"

I flicked my hand to cover yes or no so I didn't have to admit I'd been ignoring her.

"Hey, are you stealing the coins?!" One of the boys,

Jadon, was pointing at us.

"We're not," I said falteringly, before I glimpsed Alice, her hands bunched full of coins.

Unfazed, she began dropping the coins back in the water with a slow, mutinous plop-plop sound that matched her expression. "If you must know, we're following a trail to the Lake Mermaid!"

There was a chorus of sneers and sniggers, a few sarky whispers, before the group started to scatter. They were distributing small fliers across the grotto, on the Mermaid Throne and the stone window ledge, sticking them rolled up into the mouths of the larger shells.

I noticed Eleni had a stack clutched in her hand. Her brow was furrowing. "Really? You believe in mermaids now?" Sensible Grown-up.

I opened my mouth, but nothing came out. How many times had Eleni and I belittled the mermaid stories? Mocked the snap-happy tourists eagerly taking pictures of jumping fish or a patch of scaly sunlight?

Alice was staring at me too, incredulous in a different way. *Kindred spirit.* I couldn't let her down.

"I *do*," I said with an alien firmness. *Viv the Great Pretender – here to lure back tourists, save Enchanted Tails and bring Mum home.*

Eleni blinked, like she didn't recognise *that* Vivien.

Well, *good*. I was changing. New me had a beautiful new friend and lots of "likes"; new me was getting noticed by Mum. I tightened my grip on the green jewel in my hand, its sharp edges piercing my palm, just like the key to Stella's room. "And I care about the fate of Lake Splendour!" Alien firmness became fierce. I climbed out of the fountain, squelching wet feet back into socks and trainers. "Just because you haven't seen the Lake Mermaid doesn't mean she doesn't exist!"

"Don't waste your breath, Viv. They're dull mortals; they'll never be worthy of a world of magic and power," Alice was announcing regally, loud enough for the whole room.

"*Power?* What, where girls have to be deemed *beautiful* to become mermaids!" Hero hollered across the grotto. *Bat Ears.*

"And boys are mocked if they dress as mermaids!" Jadon joined in, making me think uneasily about Erik and my not wanting him to enter the Mermaid Crown in case he got laughed at. I kept forgetting to message him.

"Yeah, *because* – it's only for girls, *duh*!" Alice was snapping back. "Every girl wants to look like a mermaid! You're all just jealous!"

"Jealous?" Eleni spluttered.

"That's right. You especially – living your ordinary

life, worrying about whether you stink of chip-shop fat and clearly crushing on some girl called *Hero*."

I'd never seen Eleni's olive skin go that shade of red. She flashed me a look of hurt. "What have you been saying about me?"

I was already shaking my head, frantically trying to remember what I'd told Alice. I was sure I'd hardly mentioned Eleni, till a memory presented itself: Alice with my phone in Splash Tearooms. Had she looked through my messages?

"I'm sorry," I said to Eleni weakly.

"Do not apologise!" Alice broke in, her voice beak-sharp. "We're better than them!" She pulled at my arm, a whisper in my ear: "Grab her fliers and dump them in the water. Remember the test: *Rebellion!*"

I didn't answer her. I was still trying to find a way to tell Eleni (now bright red, hugging herself) that I hadn't said those things about her, that I never would. I could hear Alice release one of her impatient huffs. Then in one swift movement she was swiping the pile of fliers from Eleni's hands and stalking towards the grotto window. She sent them flying, doves into the air, spreading out and settling on the lake. Bad for the environment; bad for our water birds. Littering!

I was already rushing on squelchy feet to the window,

trying to grab the closest, but they were all floating away too fast.

"We're leaving," Alice was saying, more huffing as she made a fierce exit. "Now, Viv!"

Squelchy feet turned concrete; I stayed put, helplessly watching the paper doves retreat. I'd only managed to retrieve one: *Stop the Mermaid Crown or boycott the festival! Join our BIG protest march – the day before the festival!*

"What's happening to you, Vivien?" Eleni appeared next to me.

I glanced at my feet, just in case I had grown a tail. "You're the one who's changed, Eleni!" I shook the soggy flier at her. "You're going to ruin *everything*! All we have is our shop! All the village has is the Lake Mermaid!"

Hero drew up behind Eleni, sending me a withering look, like I was the bird poo on the Mermaid Girls sculpture. My other hand gripped the green jewel tighter.

"Alice is right about you!" I told Eleni, shooting purposeful evils at Hero, best-friend stealer, until she backed away. The jewel was cutting into my skin. "You don't care about me. All you care about is licking Hero's boots."

I was shaking, but I'd said it – at last; I'd told Eleni how I felt. I fixed my steely gaze back on the fliers

143

drifting away across the water; at the fog spectres in the distance, still hovering, biding their time at the base of the mountains. By the time I dared glance behind again, Eleni, everyone, had gone. No tourists, even. I was alone. Just me and a stone mermaid.

I unfurled my hand, staring again at the beautiful green stone there. *What if it* is *a gift from the Lake Mermaid? Giving me the confidence to resist Alice, to confront Eleni?* I wrapped my fingers back round it, like it was part of me now; my magical.

My phone was back insect-buzzing in my jacket pocket. Alice must have posted her film online already. A noise of squabbling ducks nearby; a hum of people enjoying the shore in the distance; the drip-drip of water from the rock ceiling; and –

"*Viv-ee-en…*"

I held my breath.

"*Viv-ee-en…*"

Faint, feathery – just like yesterday on the lake.

I turned my head slowly, a growing feeling that the mermaid right over my shoulder was no longer made of stone.

"*Viv-ee-en…*"

My concrete feet lifted. And moved. Fast. Out of the damp grotto, down the jagged tunnel, back into the yellow-grey light. My ears greedily welcoming other noises: car engines, the lap of the lake, Atlantis Arcades. But no matter how quickly I moved, I couldn't outrun the voice I'd just heard. A new feeling of dread was expanding deep inside of me ... that maybe, possibly, somehow ... there might be more to the Lake Mermaid than make-believe.

And she was watching me. She was already here.

None of These Dolls Look Like Me

Followers: 1,058. Fat lot of good it would do – Alice wasn't talking to me. I'd messaged her over the last few days reminding her we had to keep the quest going. I confided, I think I heard the Lake Mermaid, talking through her stone effigy – 'Viv-ee-en!' I told her we had to act fast, find proof to fight back against the MPs' planned protest march next Thursday – before they brought down the whole festival!

Nothing. Alice was ghosting me. A carousel of concerns was spinning through my head – with no one to share them with.

Over the weekend, the sun decided – *ah, go on then* – to put its wide-brimmed hat back on, so we became packed with day-trippers at Enchanted Tails, serving, selling, stocking shelves like it was Christmas in Lapland. *Make money while we can*, Mimi said – which is all she had time to say; if she wasn't serving customers, she was wearing creases on her forehead and worrying over her accounts ledger.

I gave the customer I was serving his change and receipt and my new false smile – less welcoming, more mermaid-smug – and clanged our old till shut again. In some ways it was good to put that eerie voice from the grotto behind me and return to predictable, humdrum life. Being around Alice was like being caught up in a tornado – exciting, but nerve-wracking. I was a whale coming up for air before I could dive back down to be with her again. *If she wants to be with you again.*

"Can you show me your most beautiful mermaid?" the next customer gushed.

It wasn't until early evening that Tinkerbell finally stopped announcing new customers and Mimi started to add up the day's takings. I took the chance to sidle over to the shop window and discreetly raise my green jewel to the light. I couldn't tell if it was precious or just coloured glass, but I'd kept it under my pillow the last couple of nights and in my pocket throughout the day. Stella had one, and now I did too. I liked to imagine it was lending me a little bit of its power, its beauty. *And –* it had given me something to message Mum about.

Wow, she'd (eventually) replied when I sent her a photo of the jewel. Then, Keep it safe – don't tell your gran – I'll get it valued for you! Which sent my heart beating racehorse-fast. To get it valued for me – well, she'd have to come and see me!

I glanced back at Mimi, worried eyes above her big black ledger as if the numbers she'd recorded were still worrying her despite a weekend of sales. Maybe if the jewel *was* precious, it might help save the shop. I clutched it tighter, ignoring the nagging doubt prodding at my chest: *It's not yours to sell.*

Mimi released a big exhale of a sigh, talking to herself. "I can't afford to give her…"

I hid my jewel back in my pocket. "Give who what?" I said directly, assertively. There she was: New Me, who spoke her mind and displeased people and did things she shouldn't. "Who do we owe money to?"

Mimi looked up, remembering I was still there. "It's

complicated." She said the last word like it was sticking in her throat.

"That's what you always say lately."

"We just need to sell more mermaids." She cast a wry smile. "Make more money."

"Money," I repeated, slowly remembering, and I bolted upstairs. I already had money. The notes Alice had sneaked into my swim bag that I'd hidden in my sock drawer. I could do something right now to help Enchanted Tails. Back downstairs, I slammed the cash down on the counter like Alice did when she'd bought the cakes. Brave, bold.

"I can help," I said proudly. Like the jewel, the money made me feel powerful. "It's a bonus from the Christofis for all my help at the chippy," I quickly lied, because Mimi was eyeing me uncertainly.

"Oh, Vivien, you are my good girl."

I felt heat rise up my face. *Good girl.*

"But this is yours." Mimi pushed it back towards me. "It belongs in your Future savings account."

A spark of annoyance; why wouldn't she let me help? "No, Mimi – we should use my savings for the shop!" *Controlling Oldies, thinking they know best!* "Anyway, what if I don't want to go to university?"

Mimi shook her head as if that was an impossibility.

"You'll be the first of our family to go. You're the future of Enchanted Tails – with you at the helm!"

"Mum didn't go to university." I screwed up my face. "And look at her."

Mimi lifted a droll eyebrow. "*Wouldn't* go – and yes, look at her." She made an even bigger in-out sigh above the counter.

The spark turned to fire. "Mum is a giant success! She's got an exciting life, she's beautiful," I reminded her. Why did she always have to be so down on Mum?

Thwack, Mimi closed the heavy ledger. "I'll put it in the bank tomorrow," she said, and slid the brown and purple notes into her moneybag. Her grimace turned to a smile. "Tell you what, let's get some air, a change of scenery. Treat ourselves to an ice cream!"

Change of scenery; maybe Mimi had been right. I'd forgotten how much fun we had when we stepped outside our shop of mermaids. It was soon pulling a curtain over my worries. We agreed Nature's Bounty's daily showcase (a bent carrot, green shoots) looked more like a crooked witch than a mermaid and Mimi insisted on giving me the flake from her 99, so we decided mine was now an emergency 999, which, *yeah*, is a *had to be there*, but it sent us into fits of giggles, as – WHAM – we almost walked right into them on the promenade.

"Viv!"

Alice.

"You!" said The Dragon beside her (as if that was my name).

Alice's eyes had started talking, lips bunching up in some kind of pleading gesture.

Mimi passed me a confused look and began manoeuvring us round, except The Dragon blocked our path. Eyes in their rice-papery skin were fixing lizard-like on me. "Why did you do it?"

"S-sorry, d-do what?" My blood began zipping pinball-fast through my veins, brain journeying at the speed of light through my recent crime travels: breaking into her dead daughter's room, stealing Stella's diary, paddling in the fountain, taking a jewel from the grotto.

"You stole from me," she narrowed it down. *The Mermaid Diary.*

Mimi made a steel-rimmed gasp. "Excuse me? My Vivien's not a thief."

The Dragon inhaled the longest breath, like she was taking in oxygen to expel fire. "Return it, please."

I flashed another look at Alice, but her talking eyes were making no sense. I made mine speak back: *You have the diary, not me!*

Meanwhile: "Vivien, what is this about?" All the colour had fled Mimi's face.

"Sixty pounds," The Dragon dispensed more fire, "to be specific."

She wasn't *talking about the diary.*

My jaw mimicked Mimi's. Sixty pounds – my half of Alice's *overdue pocket money* that she had spent on cakes and deluxe hot chocolates, and then sneaked into my swim bag.

Now sitting comfortably in Mimi's bank moneybag.

Thick, heavy tar replaced my pinball-blood. I pinched my hands together, hanging my head, a small sound at the back of my head hissing: *Deep down, you knew it was stolen.*

"Vivien?" Mimi's voice splintered. "You said that money was from the Christofis?"

I didn't understand: why wasn't Alice saying anything? Confessing?

"I'll make sure you get it back." Mimi's splintered voice was now a white flag.

But The Dragon breathed fire in return. "You'll appreciate why I cannot allow this friendship?"

Mimi nodded stiffly. "Yes," she said tight-lipped. "I do."

"Stealing, Vivien? I'm in shock. I'm spitting feathers. What *were* you thinking?" Words came out of Mimi's mouth in sharp bursts, nearly as curt and clipped as The Dragon's, the moment we were heading home – fast. I'd thrown what was left of my 999 in the bin. I felt sick. Alice had engineered it. She'd secreted the money in my swim bag not to be generous – but so I'd share the blame if she was caught out.

Angry, disappointed tears spiked my eyes. I fixed my watery gaze on the fog floating in across the lake, turning the sun into a bright silver coin, its blue misty rays like magical paths to another world I suddenly wanted to escape to. If the Lake Mermaid was real then *Call me now!*

"Alice stole it," I finally dared to say. "I thought it was her pocket money." It sounded weak even to my ears. *You knew.*

"But you told me Poseidon gave it to you!" Mimi's voice made a sound at the end, as if that lie was my worst crime.

I chewed on my bottom lip like it was a piece of rubber. I'd been so stupid. I'd let Alice lift me up – *up, up, up* – like some fantastical hot-air balloon ride, only to drop me from a great height. I rubbed at my arms as if they were actually bruised from a fall as Tinkerbell ushered us into the shop. All the dolls looked suitably smug, filled with French Revolution spectator hunger: *Not so clever now, Mimi's* good *girl!* And *my* neck on the guillotine.

"I thought I'd suggested you stay away from Alice DeLacey?" Mimi said tightly, banging her shoulder bag down on the counter so heavily the shop seemed to vibrate; china dolls clinked; the till shook.

"No, you never! You said I wasn't good enough for her." I swatted the glittery tail of the largest mermaid doll. The same one that little girl had wanted the day Alice came into the shop. I wished now I'd never met Alice.

"I did not say that. It's just Mrs DeLacey blames the village – shops like Enchanted Tails in particular – for her daughter Stella's death."

I paused. It was the first time Mimi had really mentioned Stella. *No one talked about Stella DeLacey.*

"How *did* Stella die?" I asked.

Mimi threw me a sideways glance, as if she was deciding whether I deserved an explanation, before pressing a weary hand to her jaw line. "Poor girl drowned, searching for mermaids. No one knows the details; the whole business was hushed up quickly."

I dropped myself into the purple shell beanbag. "Because of the tourists."

"Yes – that suited us all, I suppose. But it came from Mrs DeLacey. She shrouded Stella's death in mystery. We never even heard if there was a funeral." She let out a hollow sigh. "The whole affair soon became a legend in itself."

A legend.

Mimi's expression was frosting again. "But this has nothing to do with what you did! You stole sixty pounds from them, Vivien!"

"The DeLacey family have money coming out of their ears," I quoted Alice. "And you never let me have any treats or better clothes or new phones."

"So it's my fault you've turned thief?" Mimi was looking at me like I was a monster. "I don't know how to punish you – I've never *had* to punish you." She scaled frantic hands down her shiny brown plait. "You've never been bad."

I shoved my hand in my pocket, a sudden need to grip my green jewel, in case it worked like Bilbo Baggins's ring and made me invisible.

"I thought we were close. I thought we were honest with each other," Mimi was continuing. "Not like your mother."

A cracking noise. We both turned: Mum's Mermaid Crowning picture had fallen off the wall, the glass smashing. *Like she'd heard us.* "Now look what you've done!" I shouted, jumping up, as if Mimi's nagging had sent it crashing.

"Vivien, I will not have you going down Melusine's path!" Mimi talked over me, her voice louder, more urgent. "I do not want you to be like your mum," she said, loading up each of the words in case I'd not got the message yet.

I sensed my top lip tensing, curling like a wolf facing the hunter's rifle. "You're always criticising Mum. No wonder she never wants to visit!" My breath was pooling as hot and fiery as The Dragon's. "And you say we're close, but you never tell me anything about your committee meetings, about owing people money, or secrets in long metal boxes!"

And as for *them*; I stared round the roomful of self-satisfied dolls: mermaids, merrows, selkies, sirens, river nymphs, water sprites, kelpies, nixies and naiads. All staring at me with their stupid glassy eyes, their smiles wide and bright, their ridiculously silky long hair. I'd had to face them every day of my life! "We try and make money from mermaids, but you don't even believe in the Lake Mermaid!" The knots in my stomach were straightening out into sharp, pointy needles. I thought of Alice chucking all the fliers into the lake and I lunged at the worst offenders – the soft fabric mermaids lined up by the till, so *SMUG*! – sweeping them off the counter, flying through the air. I kicked out at one mermaid, sending it soaring faster, crashing into the shelf of naiad wishing dolls, toppling them over and – *crack*: over a hundred pounds' worth of china smashed on to the floor.

There was a brief moment of silence as I saw what I'd done, my tongue toying with a fast apology.

"Vivien! How could you!" Mimi got in first. "You stupid girl!"

Stupid? Actually, I wasn't sorry! Animal-fierce, I stamped my heel on to a fabric face, smiling up unperturbed. "None of these dolls look like me!" I let out in a selkie-high-pitch. "Not one!"

I was running to the door that led to our flat, stomping up the narrow staircase to our impossibly tiny home, into my shoebox of a bedroom – back into my *small* world! I slammed the door shut so the whole thin wall shook. Angry with Mimi for wanting me to be "good" all the time! Angry with Alice for betraying me! Angry with Eleni for liking Hero more than me, for choosing the Mighty Protestors over our "childish" campaigns!

But mostly – I collapsed on to my bed – I was angry with myself. For thinking I could change. *A* sparkly *tail for my dull, ordinary legs.*

I'd completely drained my eye ducts when I reached for my phone and brought up Mum's last message. I didn't follow Alice's advice this time. I didn't think about being intriguing or successful. I told Mum about Alice landing me in it and how Mimi was furious and how all she cared about was my Future savings account. When all I wanted is to be like you, Mum.

Living with me here in a proper house, with a garden sized for a trampoline and a car sized for families, just like everyone else.

Please come home, Mum. I need you.

The Final Test
and a Big Reward

Mimi went by herself to return the money to The Dragon. That night she gave me the silent treatment, except for teatime's *Pass the butter*. She didn't come in to say goodnight or to check I'd cleaned my teeth; she *always* kissed me goodnight, she *always* checked I'd brushed for two minutes.

She thought I was a monster.

I turned on to my back in bed. Maybe I was. I'd never

shouted at Mimi before; I'd never disappointed Mimi before; she'd never called me *stupid*. Knots retied in my stomach, thinking of those broken naiad wishing dolls. I was turning into someone else. Except – I jiggled my Hobbit-wide feet beneath my duvet – nope, unfortunately still me.

I felt for the green jewel under my pillow, thinking again of the voice I'd heard in the grotto, and I lifted it above my face in the dark, looking for … I don't know what. A message? I'd heard from no one else – no apology or explanation from Alice. No reply from Mum yet. I was already feeling chest-crawlingly embarrassed for that text I'd sent her. "Don't be needy, Viv," she'd said once when I was little and I didn't want her to leave after a visit. I wish I'd remembered that *before* I'd pressed send. I gripped the jewel and closed my eyes.

Stupid girl. I probably wasn't even worthy of its magic.

Monday morning, I worked in the shop while Mimi was at yet another festival meeting, probably to discuss the imminent threat from the MPs, not that she shared any of what was said when she returned. Then I went straight out, even though I didn't have swim club for an hour, to escape her disappointed eyes.

Outside, the sun was disappointed too – it had ditched its hat and cleared off, leaving the mist to stage a coup; a threatening pea-soup fog was gathering across the shore, turning Atlantis Arcades into a lighthouse beacon. I'd grabbed a handful of 2ps from my coin jar; I'd even found a bonus 10p down the back of the sofa. I just wanted to play some mindless penny drop – and maybe I'd get an inspirational message from Mermaid Messenger. Sloping inside, I found it deserted except for grumpy Ursula Undine perched toad-like in her change cabin. Though soon after I could sense her stirring behind me, no doubt checking I wasn't finding forgotten pennies in the slots. After I'd lost all my 2ps, I sloped to Mermaid Messenger. 10p in, eyes to the viewfinder, a hard pull on the lever; the beautiful mermaid floated across the viewfinder, tail turning to legs. My eyes went stupidly watery as she walked off-screen. Even an animated mermaid was abandoning me.

Clunk. Clink. I bent down to retrieve my message from the dispenser. Something like "find new friends" or "pretend none of this ever happened" would be most useful.

Not one but two pieces of paper had dropped out. I pulled out the top message: *When the wind of change arrives, some will build walls, others build windmills.*

Err, right, thanks, helpful. I reached back in for the other.

My heart seemed to come to a handbrake-stop. I recognised it instantly – it was smaller but it was the very same singed parchment. Like the bookmark in Stella's diary. Except this drawing was of a girl … in a cage. On the other side the girl had a mermaid's tail – and wings, flying out of the cage. With the words: *Find me and your wishes come true, Vivien.*

I must have made a loud gasp because I heard Ursula Undine grumble, "No refunds. I don't dispense for disappointment!"

I tucked the message safely in my bag and hurried back into the fog, my heart pulsing like a beacon. She *was* here; she *was* real. She was speaking to me. That bookmark message of Stella's – it must've come from the Lake Mermaid. And now, like the jewel, I had one too.

I wandered round the village in a fog-filled daze (even today's vegetable mermaid – a leek, green tail billowing out, blueberries for eyes – couldn't snap me out of it). I needed to share the message with someone, urgently. Mimi (unlikely), Alice (no way), Eleni (yeah, as if), Mum (still not replied).

Erik. I'd forgotten I still had Erik!

I arrived at the pool extra early, hoping to off-load to my second-best friend about *all* the strange things that were happening to me before the start of swim club. Erik would have something uplifting and reassuring to say about the strange message, for definite. Quickly changed, hair tucked into my swim cap, I hung around outside the boys' changing room, my arms protecting my bare bits – *bumpier, hairier* – and trying not to let Charlie Tate's comment bother me as he came out ("What happens if your hair touches water, Egghead? Zizzzzzzz?!").

"Erik! I need to talk to you!" I said as my ever-cheerful second-best friend eventually appeared in his trunks.

Erm, or not so-cheerful; he was frowning.

I started filling him in about Stella DeLacey and her diary first.

His frown deepened. "The girl who died searching for mermaids, who no one talks about in case the tourists hear?"

"That's the one." I nodded tightly. "If Stella *did* die." *Mimi said herself, there was no funeral!*

"And you stole her diary?"

I nodded again, a tightness in my chest at Erik's disapproving tone. He kept on walking.

"Erik?" I trotted after him, careful not to slip.

Somehow we managed to reach the middle of the dive queue for once. "Did I say something to upset you?"

"You tell me," he replied quietly. His eyes were all fidgety and blinky.

I tried searching for a reason, landing on: "Oh." Hot-chocolate-gate. Alice tagged me on our "feast" photo. "Sorry for going to Splash Tearooms without you last Monday."

Erik shook his head – like that wasn't it.

"Is it because … did Eleni tell you what happened in the Shell Grotto? She's just jealous," I burst out before I realised I was only repeating what Alice said.

Too late. "You've changed, Vivien." Erik made a loud tut. "And you'll be glad to know I've binned my costume. I won't enter the Mermaid Crown and embarrass you." He stepped away, pointing to the end of the queue. "I think I prefer it at the back."

"Suit yourself," I whispered under my breath, watching him go, a grumble in my head. *I never told him not to enter the Mermaid Crown!* and *It was only one blummin' hot chocolate!* I clutched at my exposed bits tighter, trying not to look like Billy-no-mates. I always had Erik beside me at swim club. The queue chat seemed louder somehow in the middle and it took me a while to realise Jonty was calling my name, sooner than usual. I turned quickly, too quickly, my foot skidding on a puddle of water and I tried to grab on to Erik – *Erik's not there* – before I fell in a heap on the wet floor. *Smack* – hard on my bum.

There were sniggers and giggles and there was Charlie Tate: "Swimming in puddles, Egghead?" and more laughter and my face was turning as red as my swim cap.

I think it was Sahana who reached down and offered her hand. I didn't take it; like I was going to trust *her*. I wasn't going to trust anyone ever again. I struggled up, and I went and climbed the board – and – *plop* – I did my worst forward dive ever.

I was no mermaid. That was plain for everyone to see.

The end of swim club couldn't have come sooner. I slouched out, wondering whether I was brave enough to actually *call* Mum – you know, use human voices – and apologise for my needy text and tell *her* about the Mermaid Messenger note, when –

"Viv – over here."

Alice appeared through mist like steam-engine smoke. In the same place as last time, leaning casually against the wall near the mermaid-bin, holding a packet of mermaid-hair liquorice laces.

Slowly, reluctantly, I approached her.

"You passed," she said simply, with a strange half-smile.

"You what?" I tried to give her my best sinister sneer back.

"Yesterday – I had to know you were loyal. I had to test you, to be sure."

"It was a test?" Jaw drop; eyes wide. *A test?*

"Aunt Stella said in the diary: *we must prove ourselves worthy.*" She offered me a liquorice lace.

Even though they were my favourites, I didn't take one. Right now I was torn between smacking the pack out of her hands and giving her a piece of my mind (seeing as I was getting expert at that).

Alice exhaled a musical breath like she sensed my inner tug of war. "Viv – it's just that – after the grotto incident, I felt you let me down." She pulled a half-upset, half-indignant face. "You know, sticking up for that *Eleni.*" Alice spat out her name like it tasted bad. It really shouldn't have, but it gave me a jolt of unexpected warmth: Alice was jealous of my friends.

"And then, well..." Next a dramatic horse-exhale through her nose. "Viv, I looked for the green jewel you said you'd seen in Aunt Stella's drawer. It wasn't there."

I frowned, momentarily going back to Stella's frozen-in-time bedroom. I'd definitely seen it in her drawer, I was sure. An eeriness spread through me – it was becoming commonplace – *what if it was* Stella's *green jewel nestling in my pocket?*

"And I started thinking maybe you *were* pretending, making things up."

I shook my head.

"I have a problem trusting people," Alice said in a grown-up voice, like it was an essay title. She tugged off half a lace with her front teeth. "And then The Dragon found out I'd taken money from her bedroom safe." She chewed furiously. "And I thought, well, if our pact meant anything to you, you'd share the blame. You'd prove to me I *can* trust you." She stared at me defiantly. "So I had to test you, do you see now?" She paused chewing. "Maybe I went too far."

"Maybe?"

"Here." She reached for something behind the bin. "When you pass a big test, you should always get a *big* reward."

I teetered, eyes curious. It was one of those rectangular bags made of card you get from dead posh shops, not flimsy plastic.

"Take it." She danced the bag. It had ribbons for handles.

Curiosity got the better of me. I reached for it, peeked inside. Clothes. Expensive-looking clothes.

"They're not stolen, all right? Mum gets her secretary to send me stuff all the time."

There was something else. I reached for it, not being able to stop the noise leaving my mouth. In-its-box-new; rose gold like the Princess Table all owned.

"Yeah, I got the iPhone as a gift from my dad. He keeps buying me the latest models rather than find time to see me. I've already got three," Alice added impassively.

I'd never owned anything as new and expensive, as dazzling.

"I bet your mum has an iPhone – now you can use the same emojis, FaceTime. You know, join the modern world. Give yours back to the stegosaurus you stole it from."

I didn't know what to say. Well, not true. I should refuse it, shove the bag back at Alice; tell her, *You're not forgiven*!

But then – *impress Mum* – she'd see me in those trendy clothes, photos taken with that phone.

"It's your reward for proving yourself to me, Viv. For being so courageous. And rebellious."

I could feel my cheeks wanting to glow, but my bones still felt cold. "I thought we were proving ourselves to the Lake Mermaid. Not each other."

"Same thing, isn't it?" Alice shrugged.

I pushed the bag with ribbon handles back to her (*yeah*) reluctantly. "Mimi is really angry. She's banned me from seeing you. So's your grandmother."

"And you care what they think? They're old! Past it! Don't let the Oldies decide your destiny!"

I swallowed, the taste of chlorine at my throat. I had to ask: "Alice, that naiad wishing doll you had on the boat last week – did you steal it from our shop when I first met you?"

She glanced at me, a look like she was deciding which cake to pick on the counter at Splash Tearooms. "Only by accident. I meant to pay for it. I was too embarrassed when I realised I hadn't. I just really wanted you to like me."

Alice really wanted me to like *her*?

I nodded my head regally, the way she often did.

"There's more." She indicated the bag again.

I looked back down; dug deeper. Another box, rectangular this time.

"I bought those for you with my own money. *Not* The Dragon's."

Hair straighteners.

"I confess – I sneaked a quick look at the next entry

in Stella's diary: '*Transformation*' is our last test." She came closer. I could smell her liquorice breath. "We need to make ourselves really beautiful to call the Lake Mermaid. Are you ready to transform, Viv?"

She smiled, then pulled out the diary from her shiny leather rucksack. A flick of the pages, to point at:

TEST 3: Transformation

Do you have it in you to transform yourself?

Here's your clue for how you need to change:

When the lake is lit by a full moon, face your reflection in the gloom of the cave.

Hold your precious jewel, recite the ritual, and call the Lake Mermaid.

"So we *were* meant to find the jewel?" I said.

"Clearly." Alice shut the diary. "But we're running out of time," she said, like we were on some game show where the clock was ticking. "I checked – there's a full moon in two nights' time."

She was watching me expectantly. "You're all I've got, Viv. Accept my gifts and resume the quest with me." Like my feet really were in *The Hobbit* now.

"Our followers are waiting. We must transform, together. I can't do it without you, my brave, brilliant best friend."

This time it wasn't just my cheeks glowing, but every inch of skin, outside and in, warm and pink and pleasurable. I'd not realised how much I'd missed Alice's praise. I stared down at the posh cardboard bag again. Why should I be punished by Mimi? I'd not hurt anyone. Why shouldn't I have nice things, *like everyone else*?

Alice leaned into me, her breath aniseed-bitter. "Ready to become a beautiful, powerful mermaid, Viv?"

Slowly, I began to smile. "Let's resume the quest," I agreed.

And Alice promptly nodded. Like my answer had been a test too.

We instinctively raised and crooked our pinkies, joining them so tightly my bone began to ache.

Calling the
Lake Mermaid

Full Moon Night. Three days before the start of the
Festival. Two days before the MPs' protest march to
stop the Mermaid Crown. Mimi was out at another
emergency festival meeting so it was easy to conceal:
new clothes (at last!); hair straighteners (a gift from the
gods); back being friends with Alice.

Back being friends. I'll admit, I was relieved we were
talking again. Alice was all I had now; only Alice could

understand the strange things happening to me. I'd already decided she hadn't meant to land me in it with Mimi and The Dragon – she just needed to know she could trust me. Now we were back fighting together; we were already making a difference. People were queuing up to use Atlantis Arcades' Mermaid Messenger since Alice posted about my "Lake Mermaid" magical message! And my brand-new phone (umm, that I'd not quite worked out how to use) was brightly bird-trilling (not dull insect-buzzing) hundreds of "likes" as I started getting ready. An almost-new me was emerging, butterfly-cocoon sort of thing, as I put on my new dress from Alice, covered in purple and green sequins just like a mermaid's tail (I'd never owned anything so lovely), as I slid hot irons down my hair (turning it magically past-my-shoulders straight, smoother and flick-fantastic).

Longer hair instantly made me look taller, older, more confident. I stared directly at my reflection. "*Is* there a Lake Mermaid?" I asked my bedroom mirror.

I couldn't deny something was happening … something magical. If we did find the Lake Mermaid tonight, it might make sense – I reached for my jewel – why I could swim so well. Explain why I didn't quite fit on land.

I made sure to pad out my bed with body-shaped items and I left a note on the kitchen table for Mimi: *I don't feel well. Please do not disturb.* Fat chance anyway. Mimi didn't even want to look at me right now. I'd sneak back in just past nightfall and she'd never know.

Outside the shop, the thickening fog made it appear dark already: black silhouettes of trees near the shore, a shimmery outline of a full moon forming in the grey sky. Once Alice arrived to pick me up (a tartan picnic rug under her arm), we ran – because we always ran – down the promenade, quickly past the tourist office where Mimi was having her meeting; ignoring the sign *This way to mermaid magic.* The entrance to the Shell Grotto gets locked up at night-time, so to reach the Illuminated Cave we'd have to scramble through the quarry wood – including the part that was surrounded by barbed wire.

I glanced at Alice, our running-breath mingling with mist. We were back in our own world, just me and her.

Slipping through a wall of summer leaves into the wood, we soon had to unloop our arms. Fallen trunks, a dense web of branches, and a darker grey to the air, compelled us to walk more slowly. The deeper we went, the spookier it became. A breeze was whistling through the trees like a siren. A sudden creak of wood, like an old door opening, startled me.

"I've planned for this," Alice smiled as we approached the barbed-wire boundary. The tartan picnic rug under her arm – she placed it atop the wire like a horse saddle. And she lightly vaulted over. I went next – *nope*, not as lightly – one leg dragging clumsily, a sharp prick of metal against my bare shin. I squeezed my eyes, willing myself not to imagine blood before I joined Alice on the other side.

We were in the part of the wood where no one was supposed to go. Sharp incline, untrodden ground, all kinds of forest debris making us trip, snag, stumble. Down again, alongside a large rock overhang with a caged entrance like a mouth with monster-braces. A luminous sign next to it read: *No entry! Dangerous mine!*

By the time we arrived at the now *unilluminated* Illuminated Cave, the full moon had risen higher above the lake. It created a torch-like light in the cave as we entered to a strong smell of wet stone, the drip-drip-drip of water from the black rock ceiling.

"Weirdos," Alice said as we weaved through the ten life-sized mermaid waxworks. *That did not resemble budget Dr Who baddies*; though I swore when I closed my eyes and snapped them open again, they'd moved an inch closer.

Alice began laying out her picnic rug in front of the cave's gilt-framed hologram mirror and we curled up close on the hard, damp floor, laying the diary and the green jewel in front of us. Alice also unpacked two thick church candles in holders and a box of matches. "And I made an almost-midnight feast!" she added. Crisps and biscuits and some Coke cans. She cupped her hands to light each candle, then – "See, we already look like mermaids!" she exclaimed.

I followed her gaze to the mirror: the two of us together.

My hair was almost as long and swishy as Alice's; similarly sparkly, expensive clothes; both our faces lit in sequin-green and candlelit gold. No longer ordinary-village-girl. I didn't look that out of place next to the hologram of the Lake Mermaid who was flashing on and off in the mirror. Alice started taking some photos to post, while I gratefully unwrapped a Wagon Wheel – my nerves were making me hungry.

"Do you have to think about food all the time, Viv?"

I glanced up. Alice had that steely look to her eyes behind the candlelight.

"I don't think about food all the time," I made myself argue back, mouth full of biscuit.

Alice laughed and leaned forward to hug me. "Silly, of

course you don't. But this is important; we must focus."

I nodded, but I still finished my Wagon Wheel to make a point. Alice cleared her throat and opened the diary. Turning to the next page, we began to read.

Are you there? Did you crack the clue?

I picked up my jewel; I found I needed to hold it.

Then you're ready to call the Lake Mermaid!
  1. *Recite the ritual in front of your reflection.*
  2. *Make a non-reversible blood pact that will seal your call.*
  3. *Wait for her to come.*

The words to recite were written below, along with a smudged burgundy fingerprint.

A bloody fingerprint.

My leg where I'd pricked it on the barbed wire suddenly grew sore, my stomach swelling with dissection-class nausea. So that's what Stella's earlier drawing for the "Transformation" test meant – a knife dripping with blood. I drew my arms around myself and stared about the dark, damp cave. Shivered. It suddenly appeared less magical, more macabre, like hiding in a haunted house or waiting for a vampire to wake up and bite our necks.

"That's it. The end of the diary," Alice was saying. "Let's do it."

"Do what?"

"Duh!" Alice prodded back to the two red-inked words: *blood pact.*

Bits of Wagon Wheel rose in my throat.

"Viv, we can't stop now! We'll be like blood sisters!"

"I told you, I faint at the sight of blood." I was back in biology class facing that pig's eyeball. "We don't have to do everything Stella says." Was it becoming darker in the cave? Colder? Were the waxworks getting closer?

"*Face your fears and fight to change*, Stella said!" Alice sat upright on her heels, flicking to the next page. "Let's start reciting the words." She brought one of the lit candles closer to the diary, illuminating the red ink in an old-fashioned yellow glow. I gripped my jewel tighter as I joined her, reading aloud the words; perfect, poised voices:

"We are
rebels not slaves.
We want
freedom to be who we want.
We seek

power to change.
We wish
to join you, Lake Mermaid."

I wish to join you, Mum. Please, come home soon, I added silently, briefly closing my eyes.

Opening them again, Alice was brandishing that small red penknife she'd had in the Shell Grotto last Thursday; its tip looked sharper.

Before I could stop her – "Best not to think about it" – she'd taken my little finger and pricked it, like it was something she'd done many times before.

"Ouch!" I watched a tiny bubble of blood spring up through my skin as Alice quickly pricked her own. Next, she was stamping her finger firmly against the page, steering mine to do the same, like I was a criminal.

Our bloody signatures now appeared either side of Stella's burgundy mark.

"Now we wait," Alice said, grimly satisfied, "to see if we're worthy, if she'll summon us to..." Well, I think that's the gist of what she was saying. My body had already gone biology-class-woozy, stars appearing before my eyes – *no*, definitely not the Disney-magical kind – before everything went black.

I could sense Alice's hand shaking my shoulder. "Viv, wake up!"

"What happened?" I murmured, pulling myself up on to my elbows. My right hip was hurting and I could sense an egg shape forming on the back of my head.

"I tried to catch you," Alice was saying, then she made a little yelp and her hand sprang away.

There was another noise with us in the cave: a groaning, curdling sound.

I jerked upwards into sitting. "Alice? What is that?"

"It's been here for the last few seconds." Her voice trembled. Another Alice yelp – as the candles suddenly snuffed out, sending the cave almost pitch black. "It's coming from over there," Alice exclaimed, and flew away from me.

I stumbled to standing, rubbing my skull. I could make out the shadowy shapes of the waxworks to my left – one moved; my heart leapt. "Alice, is that you?"

The figure moved again.

Heart galloping at the sound of stealthy footsteps. "Alice? Where are you?"

"Shush!" To my right, not my left. "Listen," she whispered. "Can you hear her?"

Frozen to the spot, I didn't dare look to my left again. "Listen, Viv."

Silence. Drip-drip-drip from the cave ceiling. Until –
there, I heard it again, a voice flowing as light as water.
"*Viv-ee-en. Al-ee-ce.*"

A voice that was scarily familiar.

Then – a firecracker snap: "*No return. Viv-ee-en. Al-
ee-ce.*"

Alice gasped, bundling back in against me. "It's her,
isn't it?"

We clutched at one another. I half wanted Charlie
Tate to jump out and say, "Gotcha, Egghead." The other
half wanted to be home, safe in bed, Mimi kissing me
goodnight. *Brushed your teeth, Vivien?*

"Is she coming closer?" Alice whispered, her voice
earthquaking now.

Drip-drip-drip. My whole body was rigid with wild
animal alertness, poised to run.

"*Give yourself or I take!*"

Aaargh – we both leapt from the ground.

Alice darted backwards. I could hear her trying to strike
a match, failing; eventually a yellow orb of candlelight
emerging, Alice's petrified face shining golden behind it;
deep-sea eyes, black and large.

Drip-drip-drip.

"Has she gone?" I said shakily, quietly, hopefully.

We instinctively reached for each other's hand, taking

slow steps by candlelight, towards where it seemed the voice had come from last – behind the caged sliver of a gap into the quarry mine. Where the Mermaid Girls said they went to reach the Mermaid World.

I was getting my phone-camera ready to take the picture: human legs where her shiny tail had been shed to visit us, long luscious hair, powerful body; beckoning hands... Sinister or saviour? My heart made a spasm.

Alice drew the light closer.

Nothing.

The gap in the black cave wall was empty. *Drip. Drip. Drip.*

I only spotted it as Alice circled the candle to retreat – "Wait!" – crouching to pick something up. That same familiar parchment paper. No drawing, just words this time.

"*Behind the waterfall. Journey down. Wait for me there,*" I read aloud by candlelight.

"*I will come for you,*" Alice finished with a small, urgent gasp.

"The Lake Mermaid," I said. "We called her."

Night-time had fully descended beyond the cave, the moon transformed into a bright, misty snowball, casting the wood in eerie silvery shadows. Like a film set almost.

An owl hoot; some scuttling on the forest floor. Black branches kept appearing from nowhere like gnarled fairytale figures; witch-shaped, watchful. I drew closer to Alice, our hands cupped to protect the candlelight.

"I can't believe we did it," she was repeating stupor-like, a whispery voice that somehow seemed to match the moonlit, misty woods.

I was in a trance too. "We actually called her," I joined in, though my head ached and my little finger was still throbbing for such a small pinprick of blood. I brought it up to my mouth and sucked at the skin, a metal taste like the cave smell.

Alice blew out the candle when we reached the promenade and we were almost starting to talk normally, attempting to understand what had just happened, when I was jumping out of my skin again – something grabbing at my arm.

"There you are!"

I turned to see Mimi's face, looking older, grim in the shadows.

"I get home and see you've filled your bed with clothes!" She shot a look at Alice. "And I don't suppose your grandmother knows you're out at nearly midnight either?"

A scowl formed quickly, easily, across Alice's pretty

features. "What's it got to do with you?"

"Don't let her bully you," she added to me in a whisper, and she bolted away before Mimi could stop her, disappearing down the promenade.

And I wanted to hurtle after her, to fly with her; *kindred spirits*. But Mimi's fingers were like handcuffs around my wrists. Tired, terse pupils sweeping, like The Dragon's eyes, over the new me: new clothes, new hair.

"What have you done to yourself, Vivien?"

I lifted my chin. "I've found a way to save Enchanted Tails is what I've done," I replied imperiously. A dramatic slap of my chest. "Alice and I called the Lake Mermaid! Once we get proper proof, tourists will come in their millions!"

Mimi's face turned grimmer. "Oh, Vivien, whose mirror have you been looking in?"

"The Lake Mermaid's actually! Now you Oldies can all stop playing mermaid-pretend!"

"Oldies?" Her hand gripped my wrist tighter and she started to pull me along towards the shop. "I'm fifty-two; oldie indeed. *Bed*. We'll speak about this in the morning – about how you will never see that Alice DeLacey again."

"You can't tell me what to do or who to see," I argued back, my mouth poised for some serious verbal ping-pong. I had *called* the Lake Mermaid!

"You go, girl!" another voice joined in.

I glanced around urgently, my first thought: *the Lake Mermaid, following me from the cave* – until a shadowy figure stepped out from our shop doorway: fake fur, high heels.

"Mum?"

"Hiya, Viv!"

I could hear the town clock strike the Cinderella hour as she moved under the streetlamp, her hair backlit in an angelic halo.

And my chest blazed bonfire-warm, despite the chill in the air. I'd not just called the Lake Mermaid in the caves. Somehow, by the power of our freshwater mermaid, I'd magicked my own mother home.

Wishing Mum Home

Whoa – no way.

I.

Did.

It.

I'd actually wished my mum home. A headlight beam smile spread across my face. An electric-eel charge through my body. Ordinary Village Girl? I had called the Lake Mermaid! And she'd granted my wish!

"I got the coach up from London today, been in the pub with old mates till now," Mum was answering Mimi. Her lipstick was vivid pink, her hair glistening with gold streaks under the streetlamp. Perfect; beautiful. She was like one of those Influencers the Princess Table go on about.

"I'm so glad you've come, Mum!"

"At last she speaks!" Mum said. "Haven't you grown! That hair of yours looks much better straight – more normal."

"Melusine!" Mimi snapped, and I scowled at her: Mum was praising me. Mum understood me. Not Mimi. She was too old, forbidding; too set in her ways, like Alice said.

"About time you started looking more like me – just a little bit, anyway."

"Thank you," I gushed, almost fainting from the sort-of-compliment and I lunged in for a hug, till the look on her face halted me (last visit, Mum said it was like being mauled by a hungry bear). I pecked the air around her cheek instead. She smelled of a spiky perfume, and stale-coach-journey, and wine.

"Still stinking of chlorine, Viv!" She sniffed me back. "So what's new with you?"

What's new? I grabbed a quick breath and transformed

into five-year-old me, racing round class to show off work, zero punctuation: "I won my Gold five hundred metres and Eleni and I started *Oi, Stop Your Littering!* and we collected twenty-two signatures for better school dinners and I got top marks in my history essay about '*Women who made a difference*' and Jonty says my pike reverse dive is second only to Erik's and I'm swimming in the festival Lake Race!" I took a breath. "You will stay for it, won't you?" *Please, please.*

Mum was starting to look bored.

"Best of all! I just called the Lake Mermaid! Me!"

Mum let out a bark of a laugh that clashed with a loud tut from Mimi before she was yanking Mum away from me. "Melusine, a word." Murmured ones followed, terse and growly.

"So what?" Mum was saying loudly to Mimi, a long glance at me. "Can't I change my mind?" She released an air-puff of frustration; it spiralled like smoke through the cold, damp air towards me. "My *daughter* called me. She needs me!"

My *daughter*. I was, of course, but I'd never heard her say it out loud. Full-headlight beam. I edged back towards them. "I've still got all the dolls you used to send me from your travels, Mum!" I pointed proudly up to my bedroom window above the shop.

"The what?" Mum looked blank, then: "Oh yeah, right." She pinched her pink lips at Mimi. "Viv messaged me to say she can't talk to you!"

I flinched, watching Mimi falter. "I see." Her tired eyes seemed to shrink in their sockets. "Well, now you two can spend some time together over the holidays." A zigzag breath. "But, Melusine, I decide what's best for Vivien."

"It's *Mel*. So you're still afraid the wicked witch might offer your precious princess a poisoned apple or prick her finger with a pin?"

I instinctively lifted my pinkie and sucked where Alice had drawn blood. It was throbbing again.

"Don't forget it was *you* who stole *my* daughter!" Mum laughed. A bitter, spiky laugh.

"Because you—" Mimi started, then looked sharply at me and closed her mouth again.

"You *stole* me?" I was already saying, slowly, like I was translating a foreign language. My finger was really throbbing now.

"Your gran wants you all to herself." Mum made a dramatic bow at me. "So you, Princess Viv, can be the daughter I failed to be." She jerked her head at Mimi. "She's the reason I hardly ever see you, why I cancelled my visit."

"You are?" I glowered at Mimi, my brain racing back through broken promises, forgotten birthday phone calls, abandoned trips. "You made Mum cancel?"

Mimi was rubbing at her face with both hands. "It's not as simple as that. Nothing's ever as simple as that." A long, exhausted sigh. "We'll talk in the morning, Vivien. Go on inside."

"Viv can stay with me – I'm at Neptune's Inn," Mum shot out, moving next to me.

I looked between them. Mum with her bright-pink lipstick and gold highlights and her glamorous fake-fur coat, and Mimi with her messy rope plait and bags beneath her worried eyes, her old rain jacket and wellies she must have thrown on to come and find me.

I'd always thought of her as young; suddenly she looked as old as The Dragon.

"Vivien, please, bedtime." Mimi's voice had turned pleading, a tired hand reaching out.

"You stole me?" *Lecturing me on lies and bad behaviour?* "I'm staying with my mum," I said. "And, it's *Viv*."

Viv the
All Powerful

I am Viv.

 Caller of lake mermaids.

 I climbed the steps to the diving board.

 Conjurer of lost mothers.

 No slumping; no slipping.

 Social media sensation.

 Chin up.

 Mermaid out of the water as well as in it.

Yup, mystical power was seeping through my veins like I'd ingested a magical potion. No longer frizzy-haired Vivien, abandoned by her mum. In my swimsuit I was Wonder Woman (minus the cape).

I edged towards the end of the board, glancing gazes from below; admiring, I was sure. Liberated from my egghead swim cap, because – straightened – my hair was long enough to wear in a topknot. And when the water made it frizz – well, I'd just iron it out again, now Mimi wasn't there to stop me.

Mimi.

No, don't go there. I was not going to think about the way her eyes went watery last night when she said, "Better get your toothbrush then," and "Make sure you brush for two minutes, Vivien." She only had herself to blame! *Stealing* me from Mum! I stretched my arms above my head.

Jonty had said to do a backward straight, but I felt like doing – *being* – more than that.

Viv, the all-powerful.

Palms together into an arrow, chin tuck, leap and reverse roll. I went pivoting through the air like up-river salmon. The applause was a waterfall in my ears before I even broke the surface of the pool. Everyone clapping, except for – "Show off!" (Charlie Tate) and "Not what

I asked for, Vivien." (Jonty). I didn't even go red from displeasing a teacher. Magical me just shrugged it off as I climbed out *totally* unruffled.

I returned to the place I'd claimed at the start of swim club, top of the queue, *naturally*. "Excuse me," I said to Sahana as I moved my topknot back between hers and Lily's. Naturally, I didn't trust the smile Sahana gave me, but, still, I gave her one of Alice's regal nods when she whispered, "I love your posts. You really called our Lake Mermaid?"

Erik's turn to go to the board. I could hear Charlie telling the line, under disguise of a cough, "Uh-oh, watch out for the tsunami!" and Erik winced. Something shark-like flipped inside of me. Before I knew what I was doing, I'd whipped my foot back, leg out behind Lily, snagging Charlie around the ankle like a fishhook.

Charlie not only tumbled to the floor – *result* – he slid on a puddle of water, off the side and – *splash* – into the pool.

I glanced around innocently amid a loud chorus of laughter. Even Jonty was stifling a grin under his hand.

My first *real* act of courage.

I was racing from the changing rooms with a wet topknot, eager to see Mum. She'd been too tired to talk last night. Well, apart from telling me to sleep on the floor. "No way can I share a bed with you, Viv." As I got a pillow and blankets from the wardrobe, she'd added, "You'll be all right, you've got enough padding." Which sort of made me feel like I did in my costume at swim club. But then Mum had grinned like she didn't mean it. I'd forgotten how much she loved to joke.

Reaching the foyer, though, I stalled. Erik was by the vending machine, quietly blushing as Sahana passed by with a "See you, Erik." His eyes looked smaller, sadder, as they lifted to meet mine.

"I did it for you, you know." I moved closer. "Remember?" I prompted when he didn't reply. "You said your fantasy revenge was to push Charlie into the pool?"

"Ta then, I suppose." Erik bent down to retrieve his crisps.

"Charlie had it coming," I continued in a voice like I was gangster material now as well as mermaid. *That's rock-hard Viv. Not marshmallow-soft Vivien.*

Still nothing. I frowned. "Why *are* you mad at me?"

Erik straightened up. "You really don't know?" His bottom lip gave a quiver as I pulled a blank face.

"When I messaged you – about whether it was a stupid idea to enter the Mermaid Crown – you said –" Erik paused, pulling out his phone to show me, his voice cracking as he read aloud from the screen. "*Yes, you complete dunce. Only girls can be mermaids, and beautiful ones at that.*"

"Never! I'd never use words like that!" A flush was rising fast and hot across my cheeks. "It wasn't me, Erik! Someone must have hacked my phone." I clocked the date it was sent and drew in a deep breath of chlorinated air. Alice. Sneaking a look at my old phone in Splash Tearooms, the same time she must've got the intel to shame Eleni in the Shell Grotto. *Jealous of my friends.* The idea suddenly didn't make my insides warm any more; lake-frozen instead.

"It wasn't me, I swear. I'm sorry," I added as earnestly as I could muster.

"Phew, I guess. I kept hoping it was a mistake," Erik said. He still didn't sound anything like his cheery self. "Only…" I got in step with him as he walked towards the exit. "Only I could tell you thought me entering the Crown was a daft idea."

"I just don't want you getting laughed at," I said quickly.

"No matter." Erik made a doleful shrug. "It *was* a stupid idea." He opened his crisps – our mutual favourite: salt and vinegar chipsticks. "Fancy a hot chocolate?" He offered the packet to me first. He was that kind of friend.

So I nodded. Mum had warned me not to wake her after all ("I need my beauty sleep"). We pushed on the double doors, bang into a billowing white sheet of mist outside – and:

"At last, Viv!"

Alice, cloaked in fog, was waiting in her usual place, beside the mermaid-bin.

"Hurry! We need to join the Lake Mermaid! Behind the waterfall, she said!"

"I'm off for hot chocolate with Erik," I answered bluntly. Erik was already drawing away, as if I was about to abandon him again.

"Hot chocolate! Are you mad?" Alice drew closer; tiny, forceful steps. "We've made a pact with the Lake Mermaid! You signed it with blood."

I heard Erik: "No way! Blood?"

"In all the best stories, blood pacts cannot be broken, Viv. *No return*, remember?" Her blue eyes were piercing mine, weaving their spells. For a moment there, I felt more scared of *her* hold on me than any mermaid.

"Now, let's go. Lose the Teletubby," she hissed.

My head snapped back. Like I'd just awoken from a deep sleep. Alice was no different to Charlie Tate. "How dare you call my friends nasty names!" I was hissing back. "How dare you pretend to be me and send Erik a mean message!" My stomach was suddenly a furnace, powering flames up my chest. "Come on." I turned back to Erik, ushering our feet fast down the road as Alice called out a final warning through the mist: "Who knows what happens if you break a pact with a mermaid, Viv!"

"Wow, you were dead brave back there. She scares the pants off me," Erik said, pushing the chipsticks back between us. "You really gave the Lake Mermaid your blood?"

I took a crisp to stop my teeth chattering. Alice's final words were bothering me more than I liked. "Sort of," I said, and I filled him in on what had happened in the Illuminated Cave. "But, Erik, the best bit is my mum's arrived, can you believe it? I don't need Alice. Mum can help me find the Lake Mermaid," I added proudly.

"That's wicked," Erik smiled, before: "Can you trust her?"

"My mum?" I swallowed tightly. "Or Alice?"

"Err, clearly not Alice! No – the Lake Mermaid?" His voice seemed to carry a shudder.

"I don't know." So did mine. "But the MPs have their protest tomorrow to stop the Mermaid Crown and ruin the festival. If I can just get proof we've called her … then we'll get more visitors than there are mermaid dolls!" I expanded my arms powerfully through the air, the mist immediately swallowing my hands. I dropped them back by my side. "It's the only way to save the festival, the village ... our shop."

Erik was staring thoughtfully at the chipstick in his hand. "Dad often says there's more than one way to knit a jumper."

We both considered the phrase, turning right into Lake Mermaid Road and a denser, darker fog that was transforming shopfronts and shoppers into shadows. It was like a scene from one of those eerie Victorian TV dramas. I was half expecting to hear horses' hooves and Cockney newspaper-sellers. We circled round a cluster of old people leaving Dorsal Dainties, loudly discussing the weather in crinkly voices. "'Tis a freak summer!" one exclaimed. Another said, "Course, fisherfolk of old blamed the Lake Mermaid for the fog." A third: "Aye, it was an omen that she was coming to take one of them."

The gloopy grey air seemed to slide deep inside my chest with their words, filling my lungs, as out of the corner of my eye I saw the flash of a blue cloak across the road. I paused, following the shady figure – long, tall and hooded – with narrowed eyes past Nature's Bounty, before the fog swallowed it whole. My entire body had grown as stiff as a shard of ice. *Stella's diary says mermaids wear cloaks.* I'd seen a lanky bluish outline that day on the lake. Alice said she'd seen a cloaked figure too. *Is it the Lake Mermaid?* Was she watching, waiting to snatch me, like those olden-days press gangs who seized sailors from the streets? I sped up to rejoin Erik. "I just need one good photo," I reminded myself of my mission, though my voice came out as wet as the air around me. "To fight back against the MPs."

"You know what, their protest was causing a right ole ding-dong at last night's festival committee," Erik said as we reached the misted-up window of Splash Tearooms. "Arguing over whether to meet the MPs' demands, they were, and harping on about some long metal box too."

I pulled him back from the door. "A long metal box, Erik?" It had to be the same one I caught Mimi rooting through last week.

"Uh-huh. I was there replenishing the tail pencil-toppers – they're still selling well despite the slump in tourists and—" He caught my expression and rolled his eyes apologetically. "They were talking again about the Mermaid Girls being imprisoned and getting right dramatic over this metal box of theirs." Erik blew out an old-man puff of air. "Arguing back and forth like yo-yos, they were, whether they should reveal some big secret with the village."

"Big secret?" That old postcard I'd seen Mimi with – half-woman, half-demon – was back in my head, along with the ominous omens from those old people just now, from Alice: "*Who knows what happens if you break a pact with a mermaid?*"

"Erik? What if they're hiding evidence that reveals the Lake Mermaid is really … a monster?" I blinked fast and took a quick look round in case that cloaked figure was nearby again. "A secret that might send Lake Splendour from Disney to horror film?"

"Right, like *Jaws* or that giant crocodile one?" Erik chimed. He loosened his sparkly scarf as if it was choking him.

"We need to get our hands on this metal box." I clenched both of mine tightly. "I need to know what kind of mermaid I'm dealing with."

Erik nodded decisively. "Hot chocolate can wait." He took a gulp of air as if he was going underwater. "Time to be brave, Erik."

"*Brave*, Erik?"

"I know where Dad stored the box in the tourist office." He blinked at my surprised face. "Maybe I'm changing too," he said with uncharacteristic fervour. My gangster was rubbing off on him.

Deeds Not Words

Seconds later we were sprinting away from the steamed-up window of Splash Tearooms, whizzing by Fin's Waves, bombing past Conch Curios and hurtling into the tourist office.

"My legend!" Erik's dad greeted Erik from behind the reception desk, his home-made jumper today all merfolk, knitting needles attached to the same jazzy scarf with sparkly rainbow threads.

I hung back guiltily, suddenly uneasy about what Erik's dad might think of me now, until – "Ms Vivien!" – and he began beckoning me over with the full force of his CBeebies-beam. "Am I chuffed to see you two back friends again. Cor, this Alice sounds a right troublemaker." He made serious eyes at Erik. "I've told you before, gorgeous boy, folk find fault in others when they're not happy with themselves." He flipped out his knitting needles like they'd become a sword; a woollen swish through the air. "But true friendship is the fight no one can win against." Another TV-ready grin as he made a final *click-clack-clack-click* with his needles. Pulling them out, he tied a knot in the end of the wool. "Ta-da! Early birthday present, Vivien. A summer scarf to keep you snuggly after a swim."

I'm not going to lie. Three weeks ago it would've filled me with horror to be seen wearing sparkly wool. It brings with it the high risk of unwanted attention. Now I happily wrapped the scarf round my neck. Erik's dad: he was probably the closest I'd ever get to one of my own. *Fact.*

Maybe that's why I began shaking my head as Erik mouthed, "To the stock room," behind his hand. Being bad? All of a sudden it wasn't making me feel good any more.

"I have to know the truth about the Lake Mermaid," I blurted out. "I need to see what's inside that metal box of Lydia and Violet's. *Please*. I spotted Mimi with it," I added quickly, so I didn't land Erik in it.

"You know about that, do you?" Erik's dad was frowning as much as his jolly face would allow. "Cor, that box. A thorn in the side of Lake Splendour festival committees for nigh on a century." He sucked in a breath between his teeth. "It's not easy preserving mermaid magic for the tourists."

Erik raised adult-style eyebrows. "What tourists, Dad?"

"Aye, you're right there, our Erik." Erik's dad ruffled his hair. "But with this protest afoot, the contents of that metal box have been troubling the committee more than usual."

"Why, Dad? What's in it?" Erik said, before puffing out his chest. "It could be crucial to Vivien's well-being."

Erik's dad looked between us, an expression that was more *Six O'Clock News* than children's TV. "I suppose if it's a case of the Lake Mermaid starting to give you the night frights…"

Erik was making begging hands.

"And I do keep saying to the committee, we must seek the advice of our young 'uns." He lay down his needles like a gauntlet. "I'll give you ten minutes alone with it, long enough for me to decide what I'm knitting next – *and* how to explain to the committee what I've done."

We lifted the metal lid together, releasing the smell of old things. We'd carried the box from the stock room, down the gloom of the narrow corridor – past the picture of The Little Mermaid making her tragic pact with the Sea Witch – and on into the light of Lydia and Violet's old lounge, with its bay window overlooking the lake and framing the mountains. The photographs of the Mermaid Girls seemed to inspect with us as we carefully unpacked each item:

- Violet's "*Votes for Women*" sash
- Two medals with ribbons
- An assortment of postcards
- Some ancient-looking fliers
- A folder of photographs
- Four old-fashioned train ticket stubs

"Look!" Erik said, holding up one of the ancient fliers. "A protest!"

I scanned the text. "It's advertising a suffragette march in nineteen fourteen. They held them to force

Parliament to give women the vote," I explained when Erik looked blank. "I researched suffragettes for my '*Women who made a difference*' history essay." I carefully unfolded Violet's sash. "See – purple, green and white. Suffragette stripes."

The ribbons on the medals were the same colours. I picked one up; there was a portcullis design in the middle. "*For time spent in prison*," I read out the inscription.

"So Lydia and Violet *were* criminals?" Erik exploded.

I was frowning so hard my head was starting to ache. This wasn't the story I was expecting. *Where were the mermaid secrets?*

"Vivien, look!" Erik had opened the folder of photographs and was holding a sepia print of Lydia and Violet facing a line of policemen. "They're tied to the gates of Buckingham Palace!"

Written on the other side in faded pencil writing: "*Violet and me getting arrested for chaining ourselves to the palace! After the King refused to accept our petition to grant women the VOTE!*" At the bottom, a date.

"Blimey, Vivien – it was taken when—"

"When they were with the Lake Mermaid," I finished his sentence. My hands were already reaching for the train ticket stubs. "*Departing Lake Splendour for London:*

on 16th January 1914!"

"*11th August 1914*!" Erik read out the date on the return tickets. "So when Lydia and Violet said they were in the Mermaid World, they were actually in London, getting thrown in prison!"

I hurriedly sifted through the other photographs: Lydia and Violet on marches; holding suffragette banners; working at desks. In one, they were flanking a woman who looked familiar. I flipped it over. "*Becoming 'illuminated' with Emmeline Pankhurst.*" I read out the writing and showed Erik. "The leader of the suffragettes!"

"Wowsers!"

I was already up and darting to the closest display panel, to Lydia's quote there: "*The Lake Mermaid illuminated us … tests of courage, rebellion and transformation, to find a world where deeds not words mattered.*" Why did I not make the link before?

"Erik, *Deeds not words* is the suffragette slogan. It wasn't the Lake Mermaid they were talking about *illuminating* them, it was Emmeline Pankhurst! *She* was their Lake Mermaid, their *leader*. They *did* pretend about the Mermaid World."

"Except they still travelled to another kind of world," Erik interjected diplomatically, "to join a powerful fighter – just not the fishy sort."

I stared hard at the panel photograph of both girls when they were children. "Do you think they had to hide the fact they'd run away to fight with the suffragettes because their families wouldn't approve?"

"Likely, and then they'd have to keep their prison time top secret!" Erik let out a sigh of sympathy for them.

It was a wholly different story. "Then they continued the suffragette fight back home after the war. Using a Lake Mermaid story to save the village and bring our women and girls power and independence."

Erik was nodding his head sagely. "Wise, brave, inventive Mermaid Girls," he concluded.

"Time's up, my lovelies!" Erik's dad called out from reception, and Erik started to replace everything.

"Wait!" I drew in a deep breath; there was one last thing I had to see. I picked up the pack of old postcards, shuffling quickly until I found the half-demon, half-woman with snake-like hair and fanged teeth. "*Your leader*" was scrawled in the corner; on the reverse: "*IF YOU ANSWER HER CALL TO FIGHT, YOU WILL CHANGE INTO A MONSTER LIKE HER! SHE WILL DRAG YOU DOWN AND DESTROY YOU!*" Except – it wasn't the Lake Mermaid the sender was calling a monster … but *Emmeline Pankhurst*.

It was signed by "an Englishman" – not courageous

enough to put his name to it then. I started to root through the other postcards.

One had an illustration of a princess with children seated around her, and the words: "*Women should be beautiful ornaments and contented home-makers ONLY.*"

Another was of a little girl holding a lit bomb: "*Putting the VOTE in women's and girls' hands is DANGEROUS!*"

A third was a picture of witches around a cauldron. "*Suffragettes are just bitter, ugly, jealous witches with NO husbands! They are fools who deserve imprisonment!*"

Hate-mail, all of them. There was a bitter taste growing in my mouth, something spiky and sharp expanding in my belly. I glanced briefly over at the cabinet containing our ancient queen conch shell on its pink velvet cushion. No mermaid "spoke" to Lydia and Violet through the shell. It was Emmeline Pankhurst who stirred them. So then – I shook my head to make sense of *Courage, Rebellion, Transformation* – was it just a coincidence that Stella used those same words for her three diary "tests"?

"By 'eck, Vivien, I've just thought. If the Mermaid Girls didn't find the mermaid," Erik gulped, "who is it you called in the Illuminated Cave?" His eyes grew. "What if it's the watery creature who the Romans said was Amphitrite? Or the vengeful mermaid the fisherfolk called Melusine?" He was on a roll. "Or what if she's not a mermaid at all? She might be a selkie, a siren, a leviathan?" His mouth overtook his eyes, cavernous.

Mine shrunk into a trembling, thin line. "Aren't you supposed to be helping?"

"Whoever she is, we'll face her together." Erik made a reassuring grip of my arm.

The shivers subsided just a little. "You're a really good friend," I said, and I meant it. There was nothing second about Erik. "You're the best."

I recognised that warm glow filling his round face.

If there had been a powerful potion seeping through my veins, it was starting to wear off. My legs no longer felt mermaid-light, but leaden and land-locked. Outside, the fog was swirling and thickening as I made my way back to Neptune's Inn to see Mum. I was thinking of poor Lydia and Violet thrown in prison for wanting to vote; of the anonymous, detestable hate-mail sent to suffragettes. I kept hearing Erik's words, *Who was it you called?* The possibilities circled in my head like lions around fresh meat, along with those elderly harbingers of doom from earlier: "*the fog ... omen ... coming to take one of them.*"

It was a relief, I tell you, to dart inside Neptune's Inn and get greeted by hotel staff dressed in sparkly jackets and long glossy wigs and OTT nautical furnishings. If you looked too closely you could also spot mystical dust-ball creatures and ancient maps of mould spreading across the walls. (Best not to look too closely.) I charged up the creaky wooden stairs to the room where we slept last night. I *needed* Mum more than ever, to help me decipher my mermaid mystery and decide *what next?* I opened the door – and stalled. "Mum, what are you doing?"

With the mermaid-themed curtains still drawn, she cast a shadowy Gollum shape, balled up over my wheelie suitcase. Most of my belongings were strewn across the (mermaid-themed) carpet; my washbag emptied over the (shell-shaped) bed.

"Where've you stashed this precious jewel of yours then, Viv?"

There are Monsters
to Fight on Land

My quick glance at my swim bag must have given me
away.

"In there, is it?" Mum got there before me, dragging
it off my shoulder and fumbling among my wet things
to draw it out.

"Hmm, could be precious." She was holding my jewel
in a way that felt like a fairy tale. "Or worthless. We'll
take it to a jeweller's." Her eyes changed shape before

211

they fixed on mine.

I fidgeted. I'd had a spot on my forehead since yesterday; I hoped she wasn't looking at that. "It's – it's not really mine to sell," I said finally. I'd never owned anything as special as that jewel. What if I was powerless without it?

"Nah, finders keepers," Mum said, hugging it to her chest as if *she* was the finder. "If it's a bog-standard stone, we've still got this bank account of yours. The one you mentioned in your message, yeah?" A heavy sigh, as if my silence was annoying her.

I swallowed. "That's Mimi's money, really. She's saving for my future."

"Exactly. I'm looking after *our* future together, Viv."

"Our future together?" I repeated. There was a battery-low buzzing under my skin, reminding me of my dream: me, Mum and Mimi in a proper house; garden sized for a trampoline; car sized for a family. "I've been thinking – if we convince Mimi to use my savings for Enchanted Tails we can all work together; make the shop a real family success."

"Stuff that – loss-leader that place." A sharp flick of one perfectly manicured hand. "Nah, we withdraw that money and take a long holiday, somewhere exotic. It's like the blummin' Arctic up here." Mum snapped the jewel into her handbag. "My wealth is all tied up, so to speak." Another huff through my silence. "You want me to stay, don't you? Remember your gran stole you from me!"

"She stole me," I repeated. With everything that had happened this morning, I'd almost forgotten I was cross with Mimi.

"I'm just thinking of you, Viv. Look at the state of your skin. You need sunshine, vitamin D!"

She had noticed the spot; my hand shot up to cover it. I was already disappointing her.

I did try and tell Mum about the Lake Mermaid; I tried to talk to her about Lydia and Violet's real story and the pact I'd made with an unknown mystical being (*mermaid, selkie, siren, leviathan?*), and why I had to get mermaid proof, urgently.

But Mum insisted, "Let's have some fun first!"

So I changed into one of the branded tops Alice had given me and I straightened my hair, to make Mum as proud of me as I was of her. People noticed her the moment we set out around Lake Splendour; one woman even recognised her as "Our Mermaid Crown 2001!"

I still couldn't believe she was *actually* here. That somehow I'd magically brought Mum home. I had to make it exciting for her. But it started to drizzle as we got takeaway coffee from Dorsal Dainties. "Eurgh, tastes of mud," Mum said. At Nature's Bounty I hoped she'd laugh at their aubergine mermaid, with cress for hair and seeds for eyes. She yawned. I sped her along to a poster in the window of Conch Curios advertising the festival Lake Race. "I'm going to try and win the trophy just for you, Mum!" I said, that picture in my head of Mum jumping up and down in the sunlight, cheering my triumph. Opposite me – "Of course, I won the Crown at your age" – Mum began swiping across her phone.

Drizzle turned to rain as I suggested we get a conch cream horn from Splash Tearooms. "You sure about cream, Viv? That top looks tight on you." I fiddled with my collar, pulling my top down over my tummy. *Mum just liked to joke.*

When she paused to peruse the beauty treatments on offer at Fin's Waves, I decided to try again. "Mum, if we can just get proof of a mermaid in the lake –" or, *tremble of fear*, selkie, siren, leviathan – "then we can guarantee the tourists will keep coming, whatever the MPs do."

At first I thought Mum must be frightened too, until I realised the noise from the back of her throat was laughter. "You wouldn't know we were mother and daughter. Have you seen the state of your hair, Viv?" She wasn't looking through the window of Fin's Waves, she was staring at our reflections in the glass. "We'll use some of your savings to straighten it out once and for all." She stroked a hand down her smooth golden tresses.

I touched mine. The rain had magically made it frizz again.

The floor beneath my makeshift bed felt even harder than the night before. Mum had been out drinking again, without me. She'd returned smelling of pub and perfume, and flopped straight on to the bed, making the saggy mattress sigh. Now she was snoring like a boat funnel. My stomach let out a competing groan of hunger (my dinner: the complimentary fish crackers and shell shortbread in the room) to go with its new gripes. Mum wasn't going to help; I had to face the mermaid alone.

The streetlamp was shining through the thin curtains; it kept casting watery shapes over the walls that were too easy to refashion into monsters. I lifted my head and punched my thin pillow to try and make it plumper – and – froze...

"*Viv-ee-en.*"

From outside; faint, watery...

"*Viv-ee-en.*"

215

Goosepimples popped up across my bare arms; breath quickening, fast and ragged, like I was having a nightmare.

"*Viv-ee-en, I am waiting for you.*

"*It is time to transform.*"

I shuffled my blanket cocoon to the window, peering out between the curtains. *Sharp breath.* A ghostly figure was in the alleyway directly below, indistinguishable in the swirling layers of shadows.

But the voice – both low and light – was familiar.

"*Give yourself or I take,*

"*Viv-ee-en.*

"*There is no return.*"

I shot backwards, an arm stretching out behind me to shake Mum awake. "She's here for me! What do I do?"

"Gerroff, lemme sleep." Mum slapped my hand away, dragging a pillow over her head.

My whole body quivering, I fumbled for my phone to take a photo: my proof! I could hear my heart beating like a drum in my ears.

But – she'd gone. The alleyway below was empty, as if she'd never been there.

I yanked the curtains closed again, back into my cocoon, my face against the hotel carpet and its smell of wet dog and food grease.

"*Give yourself or I take.*" The voice was in my head this time. But it was just as scary. I pulled the blanket up and over my eyes. Knees to my chest, I clung tightly to my legs as if those hands that had gripped my ankle in the lake might arrive any minute, tug me back beneath the water ... and never let go.

Two bulging yellow eyes stared up at me above a sinister pinkish smile. I attacked it with my (mermaid-shaped) knife and fork, cutting off a piece of fried egg and bacon below.

I'd not slept a wink. All night, waiting for a cloaked mermaid to slide serpent-like under the door, to crash half-human through the window, drop half-fish from the ceiling. To take me, forever. *Never to return.*

I glanced around the beamed breakfast room where there were more mermaid and Neptune waiters than tourists. "We'll make a trip to Carlisle today. Best we don't use the bank here to withdraw your savings." Opposite me, Mum tapped her nose. "Then we start our lives together, yeah."

There was no question mark at the end of her sentence. *Maybe because she never listens to my answers.*

Mum let out a cackle. "We can sort out that hair too."

"There's more important things than hair," I said

blandly, and tipped my head sideways. Funny how all of a sudden Mum looked less beautiful – though she was exactly the same. Her smile, painted on with pink felt-tip; eyes, blank as buttons, like Coraline's Other Mother.

I drew myself up straight. "You won't touch a penny of Mimi's money. You're not having the jewel."

Mum's hands immediately fled to her handbag on the table.

I was already holding it aloft when she glanced back at me.

"I took it while you were snoring this morning."

We exchanged eyes like drawn swords.

"Now, *Viv!*" Mum leaned in across the table. "We need money if you want us to be together. Isn't that what you want – like sisters, yeah?"

Sisters… Alice had said the same thing when we made our blood pact. My little finger seemed to throb again. "Did you know folklore says Melusine is a mermaid who transformed from half-snake to half-fish with two tails? The name suits you," I said (*really*, I didn't know I had it in me to sound so fiendish).

"You little madam!" Mum was already lurching across the table to the noise of chair legs screeching, a coffee cup clattering.

I didn't connect the raised hand with the sudden

shard of ice slamming against my cheek – until Mum was stammering, "N-now, let's not m-make a big deal of that, OK?"

The whole breakfast room had fallen silent. Gawping hotel guests, mermaids, Neptunes.

I gently touched my cheek, my eyes already reacting with hot tears. I'd never been hit in my entire life.

"Y-you want us to be together, don't you, Viv?"

I was already standing. "It's Vivien," I said, and my feet answered for me.

Be Your Kind of Mermaid

My slapped skin was stinging like sunburn, but I was also buzzing with a different kind of heat as I departed Neptune's Inn, like I had just escaped the cage-like clutches of the Lake Mermaid herself.

No return? Good! "I don't want to go back," I announced to myself, as cries of "Stop the Mermaid Crown!" cut through the air. Soon after they were followed by the piercing sound of whistles and horns.

Placards next, emerging through the mist; footsteps and chanting. The MP march had begun.

"Boycott the Mermaid Festival!" The fog seemed to part for swarms of students, charting a path down Lake Mermaid Road, right where the festival parade would pass tomorrow.

"*Judge us by what we do, not how we look!*" read the first placard to pass me. It was like something the suffragette leader, Emmeline Pankhurst, would shout.

More placards went by: "*Mermaids promote stereotypes!*" "*The Mermaid Crown is sexist!*" "*Halt the pressure to be pretty!*"

I no longer knew whose side I was on. I was splitting down the middle, like two halves of metal grinding noisily against one another.

Left side: Lydia and Violet fighting to grant my great-great-grandma our shop and success. *We can't stop selling mermaids!*

Versus…

Right side: Lydia and Violet fighting for women to vote, enduring prison and hate-mail; suffering for suffrage. *Yet we sell dolls that only look like the Princess Table!*

The pavement was becoming crowded as villagers and tourists paused to watch. A woman started heckling,

"The Mermaid Crown IS Lake Splendour!" Her friend joined in: "Mermaids are just a bit of fun! Who took your funny bone?" Someone else laughed, "What's wrong with a pretty mermaid!" I noticed one elderly man shaking his fist and shouting, "Leave our traditions alone! Anarchists!"

What was that phrase: *turn in your grave*? I reckon Lydia and Violet would be jumping out of theirs right now.

I stepped off the pavement into the road. *There's more than one way to knit a jumper*, Erik's dad said.

Another way was sprouting wings in my head... It involved *deeds not words*.

And that's how I found myself marching in a sea of bodies and voices. How I heard myself chanting along – "*There's all kinds of beauty besides mermaid!*" – until I heard a familiar "Vivien?" and saw Eleni making her way through to me. "What are you doing here?" Her expression looked like she was split in half too. She glanced up at her placard – "*Why don't mermaids wear glasses?*" – and fidgeted with her own spectacle frames. "I am sorry – you know – if the protest affects Enchanted Tails."

"I'm here, aren't I?" I tried an encouraging smile.

But maybe it came out skew-whiff because Eleni's

voice suddenly had a croak to it. "It's more fun campaigning with you."

And – *oh* – I had a sudden urge to tell her about Alice's nastiness and Mum slapping me and hearing the Lake Mermaid and Lydia and Violet and their true fight. It wasn't that long ago Eleni and I used to tell each other everything. But the marchers had come to an abrupt stop, placards shrouding the Mermaid Girls sculpture as if everything was all *their* fault, and I found myself sharing my idea instead – my *other way*.

I'd only just finished, when Hero began shouting from the front, "We all get a voice. Who wants to speak first?" and in a blink I heard Eleni call out, "Vivien does! Vivien has a great idea!"

And OK, I admit, I did go a tad red as everyone turned to look at me. But I also knew if I hesitated I'd stall altogether, so I let Eleni nudge me forward – "Go, go!" – and soon my (handily) broad shoulders were forging a path to the front, where the too-cool older students were lined up – Jadon, Skye, Khalil, Emma – the same ones Eleni had wanted us to sit with on the last day of school. *Now look at me.*

"There might be another way," I said, quietly at first; no one heard. I lifted myself up on to the edge of the sculpture plinth. "There might be another way,"

I shouted across the horde of heads and placards. *Deep breath.* "The village is split for and against the Mermaid Crown. One half will always be angry." Another inhale, and: "What if we keep the Mermaid Crown, but change it instead?"

"No compromises!" Hero snarled from nearby.

"She's from Enchanted Tails; she would say that," someone else shouted.

"Don't trust her – she lies!"

I turned towards the last voice, swallowing tightly. Alice: sitting nearby on the promenade wall – branded sweatshirt, frayed denim shorts; tanned legs crossed and swinging; an expression like a vengeful siren.

I put my hand on the bronze tail of Lydia for support. "It's true, the festival and Crown helps our shop." I briefly gazed up at the heads of the sculpture – that looked nothing like the pictures of the Mermaid Girls. *The real-life Lydia had short hair and one arm following the First World War; Violet had smallpox scars, a fierce scowl and her own battle wound.*

"I don't want to look like that," I declared loudly, pointing at the sculpture.

"Consider your wish granted!" It was Charlie Tate – near the front too.

"Enjoy your surprise dip yesterday, Charlie?" I

scowled, and I rose taller; a sweep of the audience with my eyes, like I'd seen speakers do on telly. "Who decides what a mermaid should look like? There's no proof to say they are long-haired and beautiful!"

I wobbled on the plinth, a sharp breath catching in my chest, because this time – heart sprinting – I caught a glimpse of blue cloak, moving through the back of the crowd; a tall, long shape, the ends of long silvery-white hair escaping its hood. I darted my eyes back to Alice, but her steely gaze was trained on me. In fact, her mouth was moving slightly, as if she was conjuring another ritual under her breath.

I quickly skimmed my eyes back to the hooded cloak. It had completely disappeared.

"Keep going, Vivien!" I heard Eleni shout.

I forced my focus back to my audience. "The Mermaid Girls were suffragettes. They used their Lake Mermaid story to change women's lives for the better." Yellow sunshine was rising up around me, cracking the fog and lending the air a marble glaze. My voice gained confidence. "To them, it wasn't about beauty or crowns, but freedom, power and change. And that's what 'Mermaid' means to me!" *Yup*, that *was* my fist punching the air.

"A mermaid doesn't need big eyes and a dainty

tail." I shook one of my wide feet.

"She doesn't have to be all sparkly! She can have short hair!" A flick at my curls.

"She can be a Goth!" Hero's friend, Skye, called out.

"A mermaid-pirate!" Emma with the diamanté eye patch.

"A parrot!" shouted Khalil, and everyone laughed. "What? I like parrots," he said earnestly.

"A Goth! A pirate! A parrot! Why not?" I shouted back.

"She can be a He!" A familiar, nervous voice called out. Erik was standing across the road by the tourist office, holding hands with his little sister, Pearl.

"Yes! Boys can be mermaids!" I called back, giving Erik a double thumbs-up at the ripple of agreement. "Tomorrow we should parade for the judges in costumes that reflect what the Lake Mermaid looks like for each of us."

"A parrot!" repeated Khalil.

"And if the judges still choose the so-called 'prettiest' mermaid and *not* the best costume?" Hero looked mockingly doubtful.

I forced my gaze not to waver from hers. "Then they're wrong and we force the Crown to be stopped."

Deeds not words. "It's what we *do* that matters!" Another raised fist.

Silence at first, until Hero started it: a Mexican wave of applause. A whoop from Eleni. A whistle from Erik. "I've always wanted to dress as a mer-parrot!" from Khalil.

I jumped down from the plinth, a new kind of *whizz-pop-banging* in my stomach as my broad shoulders started receiving hand-pats and I caught bits of excited discussions over outfits.

"I'm going to come as a four-headed fish demon," shouted one ambitious girl.

"I've always wanted to dress as the Sea Witch!" I recognised Sahana's voice.

"I'm going to sew a tail to my sister's sequin dress," said Jadon.

I heard someone repeating my words "It's what we do that matters!" and I spotted Hero climbing on to the plinth, shouting a new campaign message: "*Be YOUR kind of mermaid!*"

Mind you, it didn't stop me tripping over my big feet and stumbling as I left the crowd to reach Erik. I flourished a hand at him. "You *shall* go to the ball." He pulled an uncertain expression.

"Jadon in Year Nine is talking about borrowing his

sister's dress!" I added.

"Wow, really? Wicked," said Erik.

"You didn't really bin the costume you've been working on, did you?" I asked, more seriously.

"Nah." Erik smiled. "I was being dramatic."

"You really are changing," I said, abruptly losing my grin as Erik's finger rose grimly at something behind me. "Err, Vivien...?"

I turned, expecting to see her, the blue-hooded figure, coming for me – but it was Alice. She'd moved to the promenade wall directly across from us, standing with her penknife aloft. Its blade was catching the emerging sunlight, temporarily blinding me, as if to remind me of our pact, before she jumped down and moved away on to the shore.

Courageous,
Rebellious ... Transform

"It appears I've created a monster in you, Vivien!"
Alice said as I approached her near the water's edge. I
noticed her hands were worse than ever: nails torn and
skin shredded, scratches that were still bloody. It made
my hungry stomach turn.

"Did you see her just then, the tall figure in the blue
cloak?" I said, and Alice threw me a look of genuine
surprise.

"The Lake Mermaid?" She glanced around zealously. "Where? Let's go to her!"

I briefly checked the feathery waves, for shapes, movement, before I let out a breath. "The quest is over, Alice."

There was a new expression being drawn on Alice's face, as if a mask had slipped off. "Was that your mum I saw you with yesterday?" she said, a new layer of coolness to her voice too. "I was watching you. I always know where you are, Viv. *Always*."

"You do? How?" My mind was already filling with answers – *witchcraft, telepathy … alien abduction?* – as Alice mouthed, "Location app."

I instantly patted my pocket for my new phone. "You're tracking me?"

A flippant shrug. "I gave the phone to you, Viv. I've given you *everything* you *ever* wanted!" She began violently tugging Stella's diary out of her rucksack, sending a pen flying, before shoving it into my chest. "I think you need to read Stella's words again. The quest cannot be over. Once you start, there is no return. *Courage. Rebellion.* Now we *transform*. Or else." She sliced her penknife through the air.

Maybe it was just hearing those words that started the woodpecker of a thought – pecking at my brain.

"Those were Lydia and Violet's words – but they weren't talking about any Lake Mermaid." And I told her quickly about what Erik and I had found out about the Mermaid Girls.

Alice's eyes were losing their shine. "So they lied!" She shrugged. "It doesn't mean anything. *We* called her! And she will take if you don't give yourself!"

More familiar words, but this time from the diary. The woodpecker accelerated its pecking, prompting me to flick forward through Stella's words. Blue ink … to red ink – disguised by a different colour, but: "This isn't the same handwriting!"

I could already spy it in the twitch to Alice's eyes before I bent to retrieve the pen that had flown from her rucksack. *Red.* "*You* continued Stella's diary. *You* wrote 'My Mermaid Diary' on the front cover. *You* got the idea for the three 'tests' from the exhibition panels when I showed you round the tourist office!"

The noise from the protestors was travelling behind us; whistles and excited cries; placards bobbing happily through the evaporating mist.

"Is hopeless Watson playing confident Holmes now?" Alice was examining her shredded nails, a face like the wolf waiting for the straw house to blow down. "I only *finished* what Stella would have recorded, had she not left for the Mermaid World already!" She began to circle me, pebbles rattling beneath precise steps. "You'd never have joined me otherwise!" she said, as if I'd asked *why*. "Timid, unbelieving Vivien! I've opened your eyes to another world. You should be thanking me!"

I followed her as she spun. "The parchment messages, the voices calling my name… Was that you too, Alice?"

"You can do other things with an iPhone besides track people. If you'd not had the communication device of a stegosaurus you'd know that," she added stingingly. Then an impatient exhale like our maths teacher forced to repeat a formula. "Special apps on various devices for the distant '*Viv-ee-en*' effect. I told you I've more than one phone. Two guilty parents, remember?"

I thought of her moving around on the rowing boat; forever turning up late. "You planted the jewel in the Shell Grotto?"

"Yeah, yeah, *busted*." She pushed out both wrists together in pretence of an arrest. "I took it from Stella's drawer." A sly smile. "Face it – you're a pushover to hoodwink, Viv. You didn't even suspect it was me grabbing you in the lake. I took everything you told me about yourself – and I used it against you. I knew you'd faint in the Illuminated Cave, from one tiny prick of blood!"

She seemed to be enjoying showing off now.

"I promised that grumpy Undine woman at Atlantis Arcades free publicity if she planted the message for me in your precious Mermaid Messenger if she saw you there. I told you: money talks.

"And I stole that naiad wishing doll with glee – I wanted to see how you'd react! I got expelled from four schools for stealing!" She arched her brows proudly. "Teachers find me far too dangerous."

I flipped Stella's diary over: £9.99. "You took the price sticker from the naiad doll and put it on the diary – to make it look like it was from our shop! I knew at the time something wasn't right about that!"

Alice paused circling. "All scene-setting to reel you in, Watson. To bring you into Stella's adventure."

I could almost laugh at her cunning. "And those torn pages from the diary?"

A casual shrug. "I wasn't happy with the first draft of my story. Who is?"

I glanced back at the lake. It still didn't explain the blue cloak we'd both seen; *wisps of long silvery hair*.

All-knowing Alice seemed to guess what I was thinking. "Can't you feel it in the air? We did call her: the Lake Mermaid is waiting for us."

She still had the power to send shivers coiling up my spine.

"Stella *did* write about the waterfall!" She reached out and gripped on to my hand. "There is a cave there, Viv! I've been removing stones and rocks from its entrance for the past two weeks."

I glanced down at her shredded, bloodied fingers, now twisting into a painful Chinese burn around my skin. There was a sudden shriek from a bird of prey in the distance.

"I made you what you are today, Viv! Now it's time to give back." Her perfect features contorted like a fairground mirror. "Or I will take!"

I glanced down at the top of Alice's that I was still wearing. I suddenly really missed my second-hand anorak and my clunky old phone. I didn't care for the time it took to straighten my hair or about taking selfies with filters to make people think I looked like I didn't. I cared about what Lydia and Violet sacrificed, and picking up litter to protect our water birds. About swimming and Mimi and my friends and our shop. I pulled my hand out of her vice-like grip. "So take. I've found what I was looking for."

The *Gone to get a mermaid some lunch* sign was hanging

on the door, so I used my key, Tinkerbell welcoming me inside. Alice had left first, running away before I could hand back the green jewel, leaving me with Stella's diary.

"Mimi?" I walked steadily past the lines of mermaids, merrows, selkies, sirens, river nymphs, water sprites, kelpies, nixies and naiads; watchful eyes talking: *Ooh, lookey-here, see who's back, fishtail between her legs.*

Yeah, right – except, dolls can't talk, *can they*? Just glass, fabric, ceramic, plastic – not real.

Just dolls.

"My Vivien!" Mimi was emerging from our stock cupboard. The way she said it reminded me of Erik's dad greeting Erik – and I had to do some fast blinking. So did she.

"Mimi, I don't want her to take me," I heard myself exclaim.

"And I won't let her. Your mum texted me: she's on the next coach out of here."

I didn't correct her, tell her that I wasn't talking about Mum. I dunno – maybe I had been. "Good riddance," I tried instead.

"Ah, lovey, what's Melusine done to you?"

It must have been written in my expression or drawn still in Mum's finger marks on my cheek.

"You know what?" Mimi steered us on to the purple

shell beanbag by the window. She looked stern. "I did steal you and I'm glad I did. It was the bravest and best decision I ever made." A coy smile. "*Stole*, as in I petitioned for full custody of you."

The distant noises of the lakeside were creeping inside the shop as she gently cupped my cheek. "Truth is, your mum wasn't fit to look after you properly; hardly able to look after herself."

"She never did send the mermaids from all over the world," I stated, not asked.

"Vivien, love." A sad, sorry shake of Mimi's head. "Maybe I should've been honest with you a long time ago." She made a gesture of surrender. "I thought if I bought those dolls, stuck on some foreign stamps, it'd make you feel special. You always craved your mum's attention so much." A jerking motion of her neck, as if the next words were difficult to say. "I paid Melusine to send postcards. I used to pay her to visit, but over the last few years she's been asking for more – holding me to ransom and then cancelling last minute when I refused."

"It was Mum you were talking to about 'no more money'," I remembered sadly.

"I'm not sure what brought her in the end."

My Future savings account; Stella's jewel. "I am."

"Ah, love – what matters is that I *wished* for you with

236

all my heart." Mimi pressed her hand to her chest. I was glad for the arm that sneaked round my shoulders – a warm balm to Mum's slap, to Alice's Chinese burn. I'd missed my goodnight kisses. I *needed* telling to brush my teeth for two minutes.

Mimi made all my favourites for dinner: roast chicken and Yorkshire pudding, crispy potatoes, and gravy in our old brown teapot with the cracked spout. We sat at our small table in our tiny kitchen in our little flat and – you know what? – it suddenly felt massive; the majestic lake right outside our window. I was already in a giant's land, above a shop inspired by two powerful Mermaid Girls and run by many more.

As we ate, I told Mimi about Alice hoodwinking me and about my impromptu speech and the changes to tomorrow's parade. I left out my sightings of a hooded figure; maybe if I pretended she didn't exist, I'd stop seeing her altogether. I didn't need to explain the bit about Lydia and Violet's metal box – Erik's dad had already been on the blower, telling the committee. "He thinks we should turn the decision about the Mermaid Girls' story," Mimi said with a sigh, "over to you young 'uns."

I speared a roast potato. "Why did you hide their real

story from me?"

"Ah, lovey, I just didn't want you to feel any different to the other children here, burden you with keeping Lake Mermaid secrets from your friends."

I put my cutlery down and stared with intent at Mimi's familiar kind face, her shiny, messy rope plait. "Well, this young 'un thinks we *should* start talking about Lydia and Violet's true story – all their true trials and tests."

"But what about your future, if the tourists stop coming?" The fretting was back in Mimi's eyes. "It's not the story the visitors want, sweetheart."

"Then maybe the story needs telling differently." I glanced back out across the water – the sun was setting behind the mountains, casting a conch-shell pinky-orange that promised better weather for tomorrow's parade. "There was a legend of a mermaid here long before Lydia and Violet." Another flash of the blue cloak crept back under my skin before I reached across for Mimi's hands, dry and worn from work. She worked so hard. "Mimi, let's be courageous, rebellious … transform." The three words felt full and solid and exciting in my mouth. "It's time for Enchanted Tails to change," I finished, then: "I speak my mind these days."

"I had noticed." Mimi grinned and topped up my gravy from the teapot. "You're right –" she reached across and pinged a coil of my hair – "it should be up to you if you want to straighten your hair. And call me an Oldie again if you dare, but I do *love* your beautiful curls. Your wild and wonderful crowning glory."

Hair, see. I suppose you could say it all started with hair.

Give Yourself
or I Take

I didn't hear from Alice, or Mum, again that night. Most of the insect-buzzing from my (old) phone was about the parade. By next morning #BeYourKindofMermaid was zipping around with posts of students making last-minute parade costumes. Nearly every student was on board, according to Eleni's regular updates, and shops like Dive into Books and Nature's Bounty were creating special new displays. Mimi and I had worked well into the night too; it would be the first time I'd entered the Crown parade in three years. Come morning, I was proudly assessing the result of our hard labour in my bedroom mirror. We'd cut up one of the shop costumes, sewing purple and white tail-like frills on to the bottom of my dark-green trousers, and my purple T-shirt now dazzled with added green and white sparkles. Suffragette colours. And – ta-da – a sash just like Violet's. Except mine said: *Mer-made a difference*.

Across Lake Splendour, sunshine had brushed away the remaining strands of fog like cobwebs in an old house; it made it easier to forget all about Alice's trickery … and the sinister figure in a blue cloak. Hundreds of day-trippers and villagers were queueing at the festival huts for yummy chocolate mermaid tails and edible shell necklaces; for plastic crowns and tridents and nylon wigs. The top of the funfair's big wheel was visible from the park and there was music coming from our school's steel drum ensemble on the bandstand. Up a vehicle-free Lake Mermaid Road, fresh bunting had been strung up, uniting the shopfronts with festival fervour. And, *ahhh* – Nature's Bounty had outdone itself overnight: presenting their own *Your Kind of Mermaid* parade in a spectrum of fruit and veg imaginings. My money was on the mermaid pumpkin wearing glasses and a cheeky water-sprite expression beneath its messy, bobbed beansprout hair.

The parade itself was assembling near the shopping precinct. A melting pot of mermaid boys and Neptune girls and everyone else besides; selkies and sea monsters; Ariels and Ursulas. Goth mermaids, punk rock mermaids, beautiful sea witches. There were perfectly-pretty mermaids as well, like Princess Table Lily – and that was fine too (*"Be Your Kind of Mermaid"*).

I found Eleni handing out Poseidon's honey-sticky baklava and dressed in a mermaid-adapted version of her grandmother's traditional Greek Cypriot costume ("I've always wanted to wear it!" she'd told me last night). There were fishtails stuck to the arms of her glasses. Erik was busy admiring Dive into Books' new mermaid-diverse window (Paddington Bear looking mighty there with a marmalade tail under his sparkly duffel coat). "I love it, Erik!" I told him, checking out his papier mâché conch-shell hat sitting tall and proud on his head; tail skirt awash with holographic scales; a fine wool chain-mail top strung with scores of tiny shells. He was explaining proudly how he and his dad finished it just as shrieks and hollers erupted – the festival floats had arrived.

Not long after, the parade began, led by a float with last year's (more traditional) mermaid and Neptune winners on their thrones, flanking the cabinet that held Lake Splendour's queen conch shell – on its annual outing from the tourist office. We began moving slowly down to the lakeside, in the steps of yesterday's protest march, passing snapping press photographers. There were still some hecklers. I heard one woman shout, "Shame on you! Keep things the same!" And I nearly shouted back, *If we'd kept things the same, women wouldn't have the vote – or their own businesses!* Instead, I looked at Erik on one side of me and Eleni on the other and at Hero in front looping arms with her friends in a range of different costumes, Jadon, Emma, Skye and Khalil (yes, a mer-parrot) – and I thought of something else Erik's dad said: "No fight can win against true friendship". Somehow I already felt like a victor.

Two hours later the whole parade was lined up along the traffic-free promenade and this year's judges had noted their scores – the result would be announced tomorrow. I was thinking it had probably been the best festival parade I could remember as I made my way back to help Mimi in the shop – when I caught sight of Erik barrelling towards me, shell-hat bobbing, running-legs seriously constricted in fishtail, and breathlessly calling, "Vivien!"

My immediate thought was: *He's seen her, my monster in a blue cloak* – so I wasn't expecting, "The queen conch shell, Vivien! It's been stolen!"

Erik bent over to catch his breath. "I had to come and warn you. They think you're connected to the theft!" He pointed down the promenade to the parked float that had transported the thrones and shell cabinet – people were flocking around it – then thrust a note into my hand. "It was wrapped around the rock that smashed the glass cabinet."

Red ink, parchment paper: I knew it was from Alice before I scanned the words.

Vivien stole Stella DeLacey's diary and her precious green jewel!

She forced me to take the queen conch shell for her. Or she'll never return what's Stella's.

Take back from her. Take everything she has stolen!

And you will find the shell.

"Deidre from Conch Curios is threatening to call the police!" Erik put a reassuring hand on my arm. "What shall we do?"

I was already shaking my head. If anyone searched my room, they'd find the diary and the jewel. *So that's why she gave the diary to me yesterday.* Alice was never going to let me go.

"Tell them I'll get the shell back," I told him. I had no choice. I had to finish Stella's story.

There Once Was an Unhappy Dragon

I was running *again* – like I had been these past two weeks, when I should have been swimming and litter-picking, not chasing mermaids. I'd collected my stolen booty from my bedroom, with no time to explain to Mimi. A stitch was soon spreading from my lungs to my stomach as I flew up the steep road, instantly dreading angry village folk with pitchforks behind when I noticed the puffing noise.

"I'm not as fast as you!" Erik wheezed, catching up. "I told you: I'm helping," he added stubbornly when my face said, *Go back, Erik!* We carried on together, past the cathedral spire evergreens that kept the best view of the lake for the big houses only. A sudden wind against us, as well as Erik's costume. "Hard to run in a fishtail," he panted, doing an awkward zigzag gallop.

Reaching the wrought-iron gates, I didn't stop to think, I just hauled myself over their sharp spikes – *like I was going to wait to* not *be let in* – legs, arms, far more fluidly than last time. Erik, on the other hand: "Fishtails aren't fit for climbing," until a tear in the sparkly fabric catapulted him over.

Crunching gravel, we sped towards the lawn. The Dragon was crouched in the same position as last time, secateurs ready to snip, and Sleeping Grandpa was in the striped deckchair, the same blue cover folded neatly over his knees. "You!" was *still* my name. As if they'd been frozen in time since I last saw them.

Except – one thing had changed. "What happened to your roses?" I gasped. The canary-yellow and lavender-blue rose bushes had been flattened, as if a rebel gang of goats had just trampled on through. I could guess who ("*She loves those flowers more than me*") – Alice.

"*Why* are you here again?" she answered, black dots of

eyes pressed into papery-thin skin, pinning me down. I saw myself reflected through them: my hair a frizzy halo from the rain; my face flushed from running; trainers, still second-hand-old and dirty.

Did I care? *Nope*. "We need to find Alice. She stole the queen conch shell."

"*What?* Who is this?" Snake-like eyes inspected Erik. "A boy in a skirt?" She released a laugh as sharp as her rose thorns.

"This is Erik." Erik raised his chin high. "He's my best friend and he's helping me."

Reptilian eyes narrowed back to me. "I saw you at that mockery of a protest yesterday. I heard you make a fool of yourself." Her mean words sparked a memory of that suffragette hate-mail.

Then I spotted the thin strand of hair escaping the bound bun at her neck and a sudden puff of realisation sent me making brisk steps towards Sleeping Grandpa. I gently lifted up the blue cover on his knees, unfolding it. "Stella's cloak," I said. "*You* were there."

The Dragon's mouth was making outraged shapes.

I placed the material back down across the old man's knees. Erik was trying hard to pacify The Dragon. "It's just, Vivien's seen a sinister blue-cloaked figure in the village!" he said cheerily.

He got daggers in return. I prepared my own voice, to be kind, gentle: "Where is Stella, Mrs DeLacey? Why does she not have a grave?"

The noise The Dragon made was like a tractor engine starting; rasping, shuddering. "Ridiculous question. Why do you think?" One papery-thin hand made a wide sweeping motion, taking in the vastness of sky ... and the lively blue-green lake beneath.

"Stella was cremated," I suddenly realised. "Her ashes are in the water."

"It was what she wished for: to swim with the mermaid in the lake." A curt nod at Erik. "Each year I choose to honour the anniversary of my daughter's death by wearing her cloak."

"The hooded figure I saw was you." I confirmed what I'd already guessed, as she reached down to pick up one of the crushed lavender-blue heads on the ground.

"I was honouring my daughter Stella, retracing her steps near the lake in her mermaid cloak." A pointed inhale. "I wouldn't expect you to understand."

"But I do!" Erik burst out. "I often sleep with my mum's cardigan – since she died."

I smiled at him but The Dragon wasn't listening; those black dots were turning fiery. Quickly, I dug into my bag, feeling for the hard edges of the jewel, the diary. "These are yours." I passed them to her, catching a streak of movement in the woods beyond.

The Dragon: "Thief!"

"No – Alice tricked me," I interrupted calmly. "Alice believes Stella really became a mermaid. You need to tell her the truth."

"I do not discuss Stella with my family!" A snip of her secateurs, like a smaller snapdragon. "I certainly won't talk about her with you! It's Lake Splendour's fault Stella died! Ridiculous shops like yours making her believe in magic! Village children taunting Stella, daring her to get proof of a Lake Mermaid." Now her mouth was moving like there was something biting her tongue.

I thought of the diary and the real words from Stella that criticised her mum and blamed her sister, and I recalled another of Erik's dad's sayings: *Folk find fault in others when they're not happy with themselves.* So I tried, "You shouldn't blame yourself," which, in retrospect, was probably the worst thing you can say to a dragon. A shriek of "Out!" and I tugged Erik in the opposite direction, across the lawn and into the woods – to a backdrop of "This is private land!" and "Trespassers!" Ice, not fire, busy on her breath. I wasn't scared of her any more. She couldn't transform; she was just an unhappy dragon.

At the
Rainbow's End

She saw us coming and she moved swiftly. Of course. She wanted me to follow.

The floor of pine needles crackled and crunched as we raced after her, following threads of mist twisting through broad conifers and lanky evergreens that seemed to be on Alice's side, not ours; sturdy and imperious, like guards to DeLacey private ground.

I already knew where we were heading – even before

I caught the first roar of water.

"Aaargh!" I jolted to an abrupt halt. Alice leapt out like a nixie from behind a fir tree, hair bouncing in a tight ponytail above her head, cradling the pinky-orange conch. "If you want the shell, you'll have to come to the cave and get it!"

How had I ever thought she was magical? Like Mum, she'd put a spell on me. I'd let her.

"Just give it back, Alice!" Erik shouted, a new sternness to his voice.

"Never! I heard the Lake Mermaid through it!" she cried.

"You hear what you want to hear," retorted Erik.

Pellets of rain were starting to sneak a path between the towering foliage.

"Listen! I will call her!" Alice lifted the conch shell to her silky blonde head. Her words still had the power to make my blood chill.

"It's not a blummin' mobile phone!" And with a flip of his sparkly, torn fishtail, Erik was striking out his shell-laden chest and making a swing for the conch. Alice pushed him back hard, but Erik just returned for more. They began twirling as fast as a spinning top, Alice wearing a mask nastier than any lake leviathan and Erik growling like the sea Viking he'd been named for.

"Watch it!" I cried, following. They were heading towards the top of the waterfall. My ears were soon filling with thunderous water, the lake view expanding beneath the ledge of rock.

Erik didn't need to shout, "Vivien, help!" I was already there, my fingers prising Alice's sore ones off the shell, sending it catapulting out frisbee-style through the air, heading for the lake where it was first found. With bated breath I watched Erik leap high in the air, no longer just a water snake but a heron, balletic legs and long, strong arms and – *oof*, hands pressing it securely to his chest, just before it reached the cliff edge.

"I did it! I caught it!" – like he couldn't believe he had it in him. He passed it to me. Heavy and scratchy, it filled both my hands. Over five hundred years of mermaid-calling.

"Listen to it, Viv!" Alice cried out, her deep-sea blue eyes imploring. She really *did* believe that she'd heard something.

"Maybe you should," Erik shrugged. I made a breath of resignation – and I pressed the smooth, curved mouth against my ear. Ghostly sounds of the sea, a whirring, whistling breeze; I suppose it might be easy to shape them into words. If I needed to.

I shook my head.

"Really? You hear nothing?" Framed by today's turquoise lake, her features were creasing, skin pinkening; she was crying. They looked like real tears for once.

"Erik. Take the conch shell back; stop them panicking," I told him. "I'll be OK," I insisted, when he regarded Alice worryingly.

Alone again, I stepped towards Alice, a hand out, to show her I wasn't being unkind, as I told her about the cloak and what The Dragon said about Stella.

"She's lying!" she insisted. "The Dragon entombed the cave entrance behind the waterfall – I guessed it was her when I saw those." She pointed towards a bunch of canary-yellow and lavender-blue roses on a rock nearby. She kept shaking her head, ponytail swishing violently. "She wants to keep Stella's story and the Mermaid World to herself!"

Away from the cover of the trees, rain was falling harder.

"Let's go back and talk to her." I tried to be encouraging, because Alice's tiny steps backwards were making me nervous. She spread her torn hands palms up. "There *is* a Mermaid World. I've already seen it!" She was so close to the waterfall now, she had to shout to be heard over the deafening rush of water. "Can't I just show you?" Further steps backwards, the waterfall showering her.

"Don't make me go alone, Viv! You're my only friend."
And she turned into the roar, the ends of her golden hair
disappearing behind the watery veil as quick-footed as
that White Rabbit.

I dropped my bag and edged after her – vertigo striking
me as I glimpsed the lake below, higher than any diving
board I'd ever climbed – but she'd gone. *Hocus pocus*,
magicking herself away again. "Alice, come back!" I
began taking fairy steps along the lethally slippery stone
ledge, the curtain of water soon flattening my hair to my
scalp, clothes to my skin. Gently, patting my way along
the rock face, until I saw it: a ragged mouth in the stone.
I drew myself inside.

"I knew you wouldn't abandon me!" she exclaimed,
as soaked and skittish as a water sprite in a small, dim
cavern space. "I've another gift for you!" her voice
bounced, proudly passing me a yellow helmet, circled
with one of those torch headbands, like real cavers wear.
"I know what you're like about health and safety." She
laughed, like we knew each other back to front, like there
had been no fight; we were back on our quest, *kindred
spirits* again.

"It's not far, just through here!" She pointed her
phone torch excitedly at another gap in the cave wall.

"No – we need to leave," I said. There were shards of rock on the floor and water was leaking through crevices. "This is far too dangerous, Alice." My school hadn't forced me to watch all those cave warning videos for nothing.

"But you must see it! It's magical! A Mermaid World, I'm sure!" White Rabbit was off again – without a helmet – pushing herself through the narrow chasm. Leaving me behind like I was back on lookout duty.

I glanced towards the hole of daylight behind me, to the streams of water bleeding through cracks in the cave walls. I thought of Stella drowning in her search for mermaids, The Dragon blaming the village. I couldn't leave without Alice; we couldn't repeat Stella's tragic story. I pushed the helmet on to my sodden hair, tightening the strap and turning on its torch, and I peered into the next sliver of an opening; a slab of wet stone, descending like a tongue, smoothed slide-like by a stream of water. I climbed on and pushed off, following Alice one last time on to the rollercoaster and into the abyss.

One short, skin-scraping slide to the bottom and I fell into a crush of Alice's limbs. I spat out strands of her hair, disentangling my bones from hers. Momentarily mesmerised as my head-torch lit up an expansive chamber in an eerie golden glow.

We'd emerged under a sharp portcullis of stone that reminded me of Lydia and Violet's suffragette prison medals. Around us, stalagmites sprung like sugar cones from the ground, a limestone bluish-green. There was a pleasant musical sound of dripping and trickling. A strong scent of metal filled my nostrils.

Alice gazed with me. "I know! And look, Viv!" She urged my eyes to follow hers upwards.

Small glints of sparkling green – the colour of Stella's jewel – multiplying as my head-torch moved across the black ceiling. Star-studded, like that observatory trip we did at the start of Year Seven.

"It's the entrance to the Mermaid World!"

"It's geology," I said plainly, trying to think of the best way to convince her to scramble back up, however beautiful it all was.

"Shall we wait for the Lake Mermaid to come, Viv?" Alice asked, as if this was all my idea. "Or do we enter through there?" She was heading towards a small circle of dark water that seemed coloured by magic. I followed, the floor as wet and slippery as swimming pool tiles, directing my head-torch on to the pond, drawn with shiny greens, blues and pinks like an artist's easel.

"It's the minerals in the cave doing that to the water,"

I explained to Alice. *Not* mystical. *No* mermaids. Until – a sudden shivering beneath its oily surface sent our shrieks echoing round the chamber.

"What was that?" Heart racing, thumping.

"A mermaid!" Alice's shout echoed.

Mer-ma-aid

Mer-ma-aid

Mer-ma-aid

She began to skip round the pond – "We're here for you!" – dancing across the slippery rock like innocent stepping stones – when it all happened at once: Alice skidding, flying head first, and an iceberg-ripping eruption from behind. A river of water was gushing through the portcullis gate we'd arrived under – not rock, but another line of stalactites, now snapping off like monster teeth with a sweep of tumbling rocks. The sound and fury of a win at the penny drop.

Except it was a massive loss. As it settled, the rockfall had filled our exit almost completely.

An eerie moment of silence, then I was rushing, careful strides, towards a moaning Alice. She lifted her head with an "eurgh" sound. Blood, from a cut somewhere on her head, was turning her blonde hair burgundy. I could sense my own blood slowing, chilling. I shook my woozy head. *No*, I could not faint, not here, not now. I tugged off my *Mer-made a difference* sash. "Press it against the wound," I ordered her, quickly looking around. There had to be another way out!

"Take me to your Mermaid World," Alice was murmuring, laid out like Sleeping Beauty waiting for her wish to come true, when a sound of movement from the pond caught my ear. *Bubble. Pop.*

There *was* life in there.

I moved back towards it – all kinds of images striking up inside my head: mermaid, siren, selkie, nixie, naiad, leviathan…

…*Pike.* Our common lake fish.

It bobbed down again. I aimed my head-torch closer, illuminating the opaque blues, greens and pinks to spy a faint shaft of liquid-grey light. *It must join the lake – or a Mermaid World?* Either way, Alice needed help – I had to end this story.

Trainers and socks off *again*, as if those watery diary "tests" had all been in preparation for this, my biggest challenge yet. I took off the helmet and refastened the headband torch around my skull, catching sight of my reflection on the oily surface. *Whose mirror have you been looking in, Vivien?* That question of Mimi's suddenly swam into my head as I lowered myself into the sinister water. I knew the answer, I wanted to tell her. I knew whose story I'd been trapped inside.

Their mirror, *their* story: Mum, Alice, Charlie Tate, even our lifeless shop dolls.

My legs began a frenzied doggy-paddle – the water was deep and cold; *lake*-cold. Arms out, fingers forming an arrow, a tankful of air into my lungs and I sliced down, deep down towards the light beneath the water.

Water's my ally. In water I can be dainty and delicate, fast and fierce; I can be anything I want to be. Water turns me as regal as a swan. In water I can be a shark, a dolphin … a mermaid. Except – an ice-cold wall of resistance – now, water was the enemy. Like serpentine soldiers I had to fight; a witch I had to foil. A stronger sweep of my arms. The lake wanted to keep me and Alice here, trapped for eternity.

My lungful of oxygen was leaking as I met a spin and swirl to the water … the whirlpool! *Is this how Stella died?* Eyes stinging, I kicked harder to escape the water's clutches, to fight those serpentine soldiers, escape the cauldron-witch.

Mimi named me for the Lady of the Lake, for having powers that overcame Merlin's. I became as strong as Arthur pulling a sword from a stone. *Up-up-up*, creating my own kind of mermaid magic. To reach another world.

Lake weeds wrapping around my neck and legs,

I broke the surface gasping, blurry eyes blinded by another sudden shaft of light filled with bright colours – a vibrant, beautiful bridge of a rainbow encircling me; another magical world.

I took a greedy breath of fresh air as a different spark of light flashed white nearby, before I tore back into the water, my friend, my enemy; a fast crawl back to shore. Back into my own story.

The Festival Lake Race
One Week Later

"It's flippin' freezing!" Erik was approaching me on the sunlit shore where my bare feet were padding pebbles, limbering up for the start of the Lake Race, on the last day of festival week: swimsuit, towel … trusty swim cap. He joined me at the end of the line, his eyes drifting back to the spectators lining up on the promenade and – *double-take* – "Err, Erik, is that Sahana sending you an air kiss?"

"Oh. Yeah." Erik beamed big above his bare chest. "Yesterday, right, I told myself, *Be brave, Erik,* and I messaged Sahana." He clicked his fingers. "Turns out she's been a fan of my jumpers for a while."

"Erik, I never should have doubted you – or Sahana." I matched his beam. "You've still got your crown on, did you know?"

Erik prodded the top of his head, tutting at himself before carefully removing the sparkling tiara. He'd hardly taken it off since being crowned last Sunday. That's right, the judges (wisely, if you ask me) all voted Erik (and his brilliant costume) for this year's Mermaid Crown. His photograph, sitting on the grotto throne looking mightily regal, got featured in national newspapers. He'll go down in history as the first boy to be crowned Mermaid. Maybe the next centenary will feature an exhibition on him. For now, the festival committee are letting Erik's dad plan a new display: *Lydia and Violet, our fearless suffragettes!* There are already plans afoot to erect a new sculpture, to portray them as they really looked. And there are roles being created on the committee for student members, so they have to listen to us "young 'uns".

"Any news yet?" Erik was tilting his head at Alice's house high above the lake.

I shook mine. I'd heard nothing since Alice was rescued, except that she was OK. Her story still wasn't over, but I hope she joins our school; who knows which table she'll sit on. As for The Dragon – Mrs DeLacey – she'll have to work with the village from now on: the council is planning an exploration of the waterfall cave. Those green sparkly dots in its ceiling? *Emeralds*. Turns out the DeLaceys don't own the cave, it belongs to Lake Splendour – which is why Mrs DeLacey tried her very best to conceal it, after she found Stella's lavender-blue cloak by the magically coloured pond under a ceiling of sparkling jewels. Keeping its treasures from the world, the place where Stella met her tragic ending – and she succeeded for nearly twenty years, until Alice found her aunt's diary.

Of course, there's long been legends of emeralds buried around here. And sometimes legends are proved to be true.

I suppose you might be wondering, what of Enchanted Tails, with the truth out about the Mermaid Girls and tourists already dwindling...

Well, it's a funny thing.

See, another photo got featured in the national press. That flash of light, when I emerged from the cave beneath the rainbow bridge over the lake? Turns out it belonged to a camera of a tourist, patiently waiting for her million-dollar-mermaid shot. A spark of my trouser fishtail frills, a clever trick of head-torch, vibrant rainbow colours illuminating the waterfall, my hair, thick with weeds, swinging out and up – and hey presto, I was transformed … into our Lake Mermaid.

It first appeared online that Saturday night; by Sunday it was on the BBC website. Soon after it was spreading across global media, an image as mysterious and mystifying as P. T. Barnum's fake Fiji mermaid.

It's brought day-trippers in their droves already, snapping and searching, eating ice creams and playing penny drops; buying cream conch horns and wacky vegetables and mermaid dolls.

Kerching.

Mimi says people love a magical story. So for now we're keeping schtum about it, until we find a new direction for our shop.

"Swimmers, are you ready?" Jonty was calling the Lake Race to order. The promenade spectators began to cheer as we left our towels and stepped forward, wading into the shallows, till the cold water was pinching at our waists.

It was OK that Mum wasn't there to watch me. I looked around until I found Mimi waving; nearby was Erik's dad, Pearl on his shoulders, CBeebies-style-whooping. I glanced at Eleni waving a placard: "*Swim wild, Vivien!*" Sahana gave me a thumbs-up as well as Erik.

"Ready!"

I rolled my shoulders back. The clouds above were mottled, like mermaid scales.

"Steady!"

Pinning my eyes on our lake water that was forever changing colour; chin-up.

"Go!"

Diving, arrow straight and streamlined.

I can be anything I want in water. I can be anything I want on land.

And yes, reader ... I won.

Thank you for visiting Lake Splendour

Suffragette stories, silly vegetables and rare emeralds: there's so much more to Lake Splendour than our legendary freshwater mermaid!

Take a tour round the village and discover why our Mermaid Girls, Lydia and Violet, became inspired to join the suffragettes. Hear how they helped liberate our village girls and women. See for yourself why they chained themselves to the gates of Buckingham Palace to win women the VOTE!

Want some excitement? We're busy preparing the Emerald Cave for exploration! Book your ticket now! Or take a rowing boat out on the lake and see how many eels and pike and water birds you can spot. Next, a trip to gaze at the waterfall where fisherfolk claimed to see the Lake Mermaid – and our most recent (famous) sighting was snapped!

Hungry? Our newly refurbished Greek Cypriot restaurant, Poseidon, sells all your yummy favourites; we've no seagulls to steal your souvlaki! Or can we tempt you with some Suffragette Sponge at Splash Tearooms? Need a gift? There are replica portcullis badges, rebel icon dolls and all kinds of mermaid costumes (and we mean ALL kinds) at Enchanted Tails. Grab a bestselling souvenir pencil tail-topper at the tourist office, or seize a rebel tale from Dive into Books. Ah yes, we're about so much more than mermaids! Welcome to Lake Splendour!

P.S. Oh, and please – when you leave – do take your litter home with you.

©Lake Splendour Tourist Office

Acknowledgements

Thank you to the mystical Kirsty Stansfield for guiding me safely through the murky waters of storytelling. To Halimah, Rebecca, Sîan, Hester, Ruth and all of the talented Nosy Crow team. Also to Kathrin Honesta and the design team for yet another stunning cover!

Huge appreciation to Kate Shaw for conjuring book magic like no other. And cheers, my invaluable early readers: Lucy, Joy, Emily. Thanks also to Christina and Eleni for your stories, and your name! And to a few notable cheerleaders: Campbell and Newhall clans, Sally, Arshi, Harprit, Helen, Dougie, my book club, fellow local and online authors, the ever-supportive Twitter crowd, and old and new friends for all your kindness (I hope you know who you are).

A final rowdy applause for my dearest Duncs and marvellous Mae, for reading anything I push under your noses, and to my maverick Laurie … this book is for you, and your wild and wonderful hair.

Glossary of Merfolk and Water Beings

Mermaid: half-woman and half-fish

Merman: half-man and half-fish

Merrow: Irish mermaid who warned fisherfolk of approaching storms

Selkie: a seal-like creature that turns human on land

Siren: half-woman, half-bird from Greek mythology, enticing voyagers by their beautiful singing

River nymph: river divinity who lives thousands of years

Water sprite: excitable guardian of water

Kelpie: Scottish folklore spirit of the waters in the form of a horse

Nixie: a water wraith inhabiting lakes, rivers, waterfalls and the sea, sometimes half-child or half-horse

Naiad: a nymph of lake, rivers and streams

Leviathan: a monster of the waters

Neptune: Roman god of the sea, carries a trident

Amphitrite: Greek goddess of the sea

Poseidon: Greek god of the sea

Undine: spirit of the waters, created without a soul

Melusine: mermaid who transformed from half-snake to half-fish with two tails

Erik: Norse navigator who explored Greenland

Vivien: Lady of the Lake, who gave and received the sword of Excalibur